Now that the weather is [...] the sun with this month's collection of seductive reads from Harlequin Presents!

Favorite author Lucy Monroe brings you *Bought: The Greek's Bride,* the first installment in her MEDITERRANEAN BRIDES duet. Two billionaires are out to claim their brides—but have they met their match? Read Sandor's story now and Miguel's next month! Meanwhile, Miranda Lee's *The Ruthless Marriage Proposal* is the sensuous tale of a housekeeper who falls in love with her handsome billionaire boss.

If it's a sexy sheikh you're after, *The Sultan's Virgin Bride* by Sarah Morgan has a ruthless sultan determined to have the one woman he can't. In Kim Lawrence's *The Italian's Wedding Ultimatum* an Italian's seduction leads to passion and pregnancy! The international theme continues with *Kept by the Spanish Billionaire* by Cathy Williams, where playboy Rafael Vives is shocked when his mistress of the moment turns out to be much more.

In Robyn Donald's *The Blackmail Bargain* Curt blackmails Peta, unaware that she's a penniless virgin. And Lee Wilkinson's *Wife by Approval* is the story of a handsome wealthy heir who needs glamorous Valentina to secure his birthright.

Finally, there's Natalie Rivers with her debut novel, *The Kristallis Baby,* where an arrogant Greek tycoon claims his orphaned nephew—by taking virginal Carrie's innocence and wedding her. Happy reading!

Surrender To The Sheikh

*He's proud, passionate, primal—
dare she surrender to the sheikh?*

Feel warm winds blowing through your hair
and the hot desert sun on your skin
as you are transported to exotic lands....
As the temperature rises, let yourself be seduced
by our sexy, irresistible sheikhs.

If you love our men of the desert,
look for more stories coming soon
in this enthralling miniseries:

In July look out for
The Sheikh's Ransomed Bride
by Annie West

Sarah Morgan

THE SULTAN'S VIRGIN BRIDE

Surrender To The Sheikh

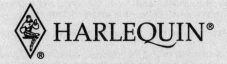

HARLEQUIN®

TORONTO • NEW YORK • LONDON
AMSTERDAM • PARIS • SYDNEY • HAMBURG
STOCKHOLM • ATHENS • TOKYO • MILAN • MADRID
PRAGUE • WARSAW • BUDAPEST • AUCKLAND

ISBN-13: 978-0-373-12637-8
ISBN-10: 0-373-12637-9

THE SULTAN'S VIRGIN BRIDE

First North American Publication 2007.

Copyright © 2006 by Sarah Morgan.

www.eHarlequin.com

Printed in U.S.A.

All about the author...
Sarah Morgan

SARAH MORGAN was born in Wiltshire and started writing at the age of eight when she produced an autobiography of her hamster.

At the age of eighteen she traveled to London to train as a nurse in one of London's top teaching hospitals, and she describes what happened in those years as extremely happy and definitely censored! She worked in a number of areas in the hospital after she qualified.

Over time her writing interests had moved on from hamsters to men, and she started creating romance fiction. Her first completed manuscript, written after the birth of her first child, was rejected by Harlequin, but the comments were encouraging, so she tried again; on the third attempt her manuscript *Worth the Risk* was accepted unchanged. She describes receiving the acceptance letter as one of the best moments of her life, after meeting her husband and having her two children.

Sarah still works part-time in a health-related industry and spends the rest of the time with her family trying to squeeze in writing whenever she can. She is an enthusiastic skier and walker, and she loves outdoor life.

For Nicola Cornick, whose books I love
and whose friendship I value.

CHAPTER ONE

EVERYTHING was in place.

Like a predator he lay in wait, his powerful body still and his eyes alert and watchful.

Remote and unapproachable, Sultan Tariq bin Omar al-Sharma lounged silently in his chair and surveyed the ballroom from the best table in the room. The arrogant tilt of his proud head and the cynical glint in his cold dark eyes were sufficient to keep people at a respectful distance. As an additional precaution, bodyguards hovered in the background, ready to apprehend anyone brave or foolish enough to approach.

Tariq ignored them in the same way that he ignored the stares of everyone in the room, accepting the attention with the bored indifference of someone who had been the object of interest and speculation since birth.

He was the most eligible bachelor in the world, relentlessly pursued by scores of hopeful women. A man of strength and power, hard and tough and almost indecently handsome.

In a room filled with powerful, successful men, Tariq was the ultimate catch and the buzz of interest built to fever pitch. Women cast covetous glances in his direction, each one indulging in her own personal fantasy about being the one to draw his eye because to do so would be the romantic equivalent of winning the lottery.

Ordinarily he might have exploited that appeal to ruthless advantage, but tonight he was interested in only one woman.

And so far she hadn't arrived.

Nothing about his powerful, athletic frame suggested that his presence in the room stemmed from anything other than a desire to patronize a high profile charity ball. His handsome, aristocratic face was devoid of expression, giving no hint that this evening was the culmination of months of meticulous planning.

For him, tonight was all about business.

He needed control of the Tyndall Pipeline Corporation. The construction of the pipeline was essential to the successful future of Tazkash—crucial for the security and prosperity of his people. He needed to pump oil across the desert. The project was economically, environmentally and financially viable. Everything was in place.

But Harrison Tyndall, Chief Executive Officer, wasn't playing ball. He wasn't even willing to negotiate. And Tariq knew the reason why.

The girl.

Farrah Tyndall.

Daddy's baby. Spoiled little rich girl. Party girl. 'It' girl. The girl who'd always had everything she wanted.

Except him.

Tariq's hard mouth curved into a smile. She *could* have had him, he recalled. But she hadn't liked his terms.

And Harrison Tyndall hadn't liked them either. Weeks of delicate negotiation between the state of Tazkash and the Tyndall Pipeline Corporation had broken down and there had been no further communication on the subject for five long years.

It was a sorry state of affairs, Tariq mused silently, when the wishes of a woman dictated the flow of business.

Seated at his elbow, Hasim Akbar, his Minister for Oil Exports, cleared his throat respectfully. 'Perhaps I should walk around the room, Your Excellency. See if the Tyndall girl has arrived yet.'

'She hasn't arrived.' Tariq spoke in a lazy drawl, his fluent, perfectly accented English the product of the most expensive education money could buy. 'If she were here, I would know.'

Hasim tapped his fingers on the table, unable to conceal his mounting anxiety. 'Then she is *extremely* late.'

Tariq gave a faint smile. 'Of course she is extremely late. To be on time or even slightly late would be a wasted opportunity.'

He had no doubt that Farrah Tyndall was currently loitering in the wings somewhere, poised to make her entrance as dramatic as possible. After all, wasn't socializing the entire focus of her shallow, pampered existence? Having spent all day with her hairdresser and her stylist, she would be more than ready to display the fruits of their labour. Living up to her mother's reputation. Farrah Tyndall was just like every other woman he'd ever had dealings with. She cared about nothing more important than shoes, hair and the state of her nails.

'It is getting late. Maybe she's here somewhere,' Hasim suggested nervously, 'but we just haven't noticed her.'

'Clearly you've never seen a picture of Farrah Tyndall.' Tariq turned his head, a slightly cynical inflection to his tone as he surveyed the man next to him. 'If you had, then you would know that being noticed is the one thing she does really, *really* well.'

'She is beautiful?'

'Sublime.' Tariq's gaze slid back to the head of the staircase. 'Farrah Tyndall can light up a room with one smile from her perfectly painted mouth. If she were already here then the men in the room would be glued to the spot and staring.'

As he had stared on that first day, standing on the beach at the desert camp of Nazaar.

Her beauty was enough to blind a man. *Enough to blind him to her truly shallow nature.*

But it wasn't her beauty or her personality that interested him now. For the past few months his staff had been dis-creetly buying every available share in the Tyndall Pipeline Corporation. Control was finally within his reach. All he needed to take over the company and guarantee the pipeline project was a further twenty per cent.

And Farrah Tyndall owned twenty per cent.

Hasim was breathing rapidly. 'I still think this plan is impossible.'

Tariq gave a slow smile, totally unperturbed. 'The challenge and stimulation of business comes from making the impossible possible,' he observed, his long fingers toying idly with the stem of his glass, 'and to find a solution where there appears to be none.'

'But if you carry out your plan then you will have to *marry* her—'

Confronted by that unpalatable truth, Tariq's fingers tightened on the glass. Despite his outward display of indifference, his internal reaction to the prospect of marriage bordered on the allergic. 'Only in the short term,' he drawled and Hasim's expression transformed from mild concern to one of extreme anxiety.

'You are seriously considering invoking the ancient law that allows you to divorce after forty days and forty nights?'

'Everything my wife owns, and I do mean *everything*,' Tariq inserted with silken emphasis, 'becomes mine on marriage. I want those shares but I have no wish to stay married.'

The plan was perfect. Masterly.

Hasim fiddled nervously with the cloth of his suit. 'To the best of my knowledge, that particular divorce law has not been applied for centuries.'

'And most people have forgotten its existence, which is clearly to our advantage.'

'It is an insult to a bride and her family, Your Excellency.' Hasim's voice was hoarse and Tariq lifted an ebony brow.

'How is it possible to insult a woman who thinks only of partying and possessions?' His tone was sardonic. 'If you're expecting me to feel sorry for Farrah Tyndall then you're wasting your time.'

'But what if she doesn't come tonight? *Everything* depends on the girl.' The Minister shifted on his chair, beads of sweat standing out on his brow as the prolonged wait started to affect his nerves.

By contrast Tariq, who had nerves of steel and had never doubted his own abilities, sat relaxed and confident, his gaze still focused on the sweep of stairs that led down into the ballroom. 'She will come. Her father is patron of this charity and she's never been one to miss a good party. You can safely leave the girl to me, Hasim.'

And even as he said the words she appeared at the top of the staircase.

Poised like a princess, her golden hair piled high on her head in a style no doubt selected in order to display her long slender neck to greatest advantage, the dress a sheath of glittering gold falling from neck to ankles and hugging a body that was nothing short of female perfection.

Clearly he'd been right in his assumption that she'd spent the entire afternoon at the hairdresser and with her stylist, Tariq thought with cold objectivity, his expert gaze sliding slowly down her body.

Which meant that her priorities hadn't changed at all in the five years since they'd last met.

But there were changes, he noticed, as he watched the way she drifted down the stairs with the effortless grace of a dancer. She carried herself differently. No longer the leggy teenager who had appeared slightly awkward and self-conscious, she'd developed poise and sophistication. She'd grown into her stunning looks.

The girl he'd once known had become a woman.

Although he was careful to betray nothing, he felt everything inside him tighten in a vicious attack of lust. Desire, hot and fierce, gripped his lean, athletic frame and, for a moment, he was sorely tempted to drag her from the ballroom and make use of the nearest available flat surface.

Which just went to prove, he thought grimly, that the male libido was no judge of character and completely disconnected from the brain.

Irritated by the violence of his own response to her, he watched in brooding silence as she weaved between tables, pausing occasionally to meet and greet. Her smile was an intriguing mix of allure and innocence and she used it well, captivating her male audience with the gentle curve of her lips and the teasing flash of her eyes.

She was an accomplished flirt. A woman of exceptional beauty who knew exactly how to use the gifts that nature had bestowed upon her to best advantage. And she used each gift to its full as she worked the room, shining brighter than any star as she moved towards her table with a group of friends.

Her table was next to his. He knew that because his instructions to his staff had been quite specific and, like a jungle cat lying in wait for its prey, Tariq remained still, poised for her to notice him.

The tension inside him rose and anticipation thrummed in his veins.

Any moment now…

She exchanged a few words with a passing male, who laughed and kissed her hand. Then she dropped her tiny bag on the table and turned, the smile still on her lips.

And saw him.

The colour drained from her beautiful face and the bright smile died instantly like a vibrant flame doused by cold water.

Something vulnerable flared in the depths of her amazing green eyes and, for a brief moment, the woman vanished and he saw the girl again.

She looked like someone who had sustained a severe shock

and then she dragged her gaze away from his, closed her fingers over the back of the chair to steady herself and took several deep breaths.

Observing the effect his presence had on her with arrogant masculine satisfaction, Tariq reflected on the fact that his task was going to be every bit as easy as he'd imagined it would be.

Simple.

He watched as she straightened her narrow shoulders and let her hands fall from the chair that she'd used for support. Her eyes blank of expression, she looked at him, inclined her head gracefully in his direction and then turned back to her friends, nothing in her demeanour suggesting that he was anything other than the most casual of acquaintances.

Playing it cool.

His gaze lingered on the soft swell of her breasts and he reflected that, although he had a personal rule of never mixing business with pleasure, he had no objection to indulging in pleasure once the business was over. And, although his marriage to the Tyndall heiress was business, the wedding night would most *definitely* be his pleasure.

Forty days and forty nights of pleasure, to be exact. With a clear mental vision of how he intended to pass his limited time as a married man, Tariq gave a slow smile of anticipation.

It appeared as though this business deal would not be anything like the arduous task that he'd initially imagined.

Marriage had suddenly taken on an appeal that had previously escaped him.

She had to get away.

Farrah stood in a dark corner of the terrace overlooking the manicured grounds. The rain had long since stopped and the August night was warm and muggy, but she was shivering like a whippet. She ran her hands up and down her arms in an attempt to warm herself but it made no difference. The chill was deep inside her. If there had been any way of leaving without her absence being noted she would have done so because to stay in the same room as Tariq bin Omar al-Sharma was nothing short of agony.

She hadn't even known he was in the country.

Had she known, she would have stayed at home, she would have gone abroad, *she would have dug a hole and hidden—* anything other than risk finding herself face to face with him. Especially with no warning. No chance to prepare herself mentally for the anguish of seeing him again.

One glance from those exotic dark eyes and she'd turned into a schoolgirl again. An awkward, wide-eyed, besotted teenager, weighed down by more insecurities than she could count.

She hadn't been good enough for him.

He'd taken her fragile, fledgling self-confidence and ground it into the dust. Misery and humiliation mingled inside her and she wanted to curl up in a dark corner and hide herself away until she was sure he'd flown back to Tazkash.

People always said that you could leave your past behind, but what were you supposed to do when your past had his own fleet of private planes and could follow you anywhere?

Dinner had proved a long drawn out ordeal, an exercise in restraint and endurance, as she'd talked and laughed in a determined attempt not to reveal her distress to her companions. And all the time she'd been aware of him.

Fate had seated her with her back to him and yet it had made no difference. She'd been able to feel the power of his presence. *Feel his dark gaze burning into her back.* And in the end, unable to sit a moment longer, she'd made her excuses and slipped outside.

It was odd, she thought dully, that however much you changed yourself on the outside, the inside stayed the same. No matter how glossy the outside, inside lay all the old insecurities. Inside she was still the same gawky, awkward, overweight girl who didn't look right, wasn't interested in the right things and was a massive disappointment to her glamorous mother.

Memories of her mother intensified her misery and she lifted a shaking hand to her throbbing head. It had been six years since her mother's death, but the desperate desire to please, *to make her mother proud*, still lingered. She felt herself unravelling and suddenly she knew how Cinderella must have felt as the clock struck midnight. If she didn't escape then all would be revealed. People might catch a glimpse of the real Farrah Tyndall and she owed it to her mother's memory not to let that happen. *She needed to go home, where she could be herself, without witnesses.*

She heard laughter from the ballroom and then footsteps, a purposeful masculine tread, and she stiffened her shoulders, trying to make clear from her body language that she sought neither company nor conversation.

'It's unlike you to miss a party, Farrah.'

His voice came from behind her, deep, silky and unmistakably male, and everything in her tensed in response.

Once she'd loved his voice. She'd found his smooth, mellifluous tones both exotic and seductive.

She'd found everything about him exotic and seductive.

They called him the Desert Prince and the name had stuck, despite the fact that he'd been the ruler of Tazkash for the past four years and was now Sultan. And, Prince or Sultan, Tariq bin Omar al-Sharma was a brilliant businessman. Fearless and aggressive, as Crown Prince he'd transformed the fortunes of a small, insignificant state and turned Tazkash into a major player in the world markets. As Sultan he'd earned the respect of politicians and business institutions.

He spoke and people listened.

Now the sound of his voice transported her to the very edge of a panic attack.

Part of her wanted to ignore him, wanted to deny him the satisfaction of knowing that she even remembered him, and part of her wanted to turn and hurt him. *Hurt him as much as he had hurt her with his cruel rejection.*

Fortunately she'd been taught that it was best never to reveal one's true feelings and her tutor in that lesson had been Tariq himself. He was a man who revealed nothing. She was ruled by her emotions and he was ruled by his mind.

She'd shown. He'd mocked. She'd learned.

Remembering the harsh lesson, she turned slowly, determined to behave as if his presence meant nothing more than an unwarranted disturbance. They were as different as it was possible for two people to be. And he'd made it painfully clear that she didn't belong in his world.

'Your Highness.' Her voice was stiff and ferociously polite and she was careful not to look directly at him. *To look into those eyes was to risk falling and she had no intention of falling.* A glance behind him told her that they were alone on the terrace although she saw a bulky shadow in the doorway, which she took to be that of a bodyguard. They were never far from him, a constant reminder of his wealth and importance. 'I find it warm in the ballroom.'

'And yet you are shivering.' With an economy of movement that was so much a part of the man, he stepped closer and panic shot through her.

Her throat dried and her fingers tightened around her jewelled evening bag, although why, she had no idea. The richest, most eligible man in the world was hardly likely to be planning to steal her possessions. And anyway, she thought dully, he'd already stolen the only part of herself she'd ever valued. *Her heart.*

Determined to send him on his way, she glanced up and immediately regretted the impulse.

His shockingly handsome face was both familiar and alien. When she'd known him, at the beginning at least, she'd always seen humour and warmth behind the cool exterior that he chose to present to the world. It hadn't taken her long to realise that she'd seen what she wanted to see. Looking at him now, she saw nothing that wasn't tough and hard.

'Let's not play games, Your Excellency.' She was proud of herself for keeping her voice steady. *For behaving with restraint.* 'We find ourselves at the same event and that is an unhappy coincidence for both of us, but that certainly doesn't mean we have to spend time together. We have no need to pretend a friendship that we both know does not exist.'

He looked spectacular in a formal dinner jacket, she thought absently. As spectacular as he did dressed in more traditional robes. And she knew him to be equally comfortable in either. Tariq moved between cultures with the ease and confidence that others less skilled and adaptable could only envy.

He was *totally* out of her league and the fact that she'd once believed that they could have a future together was a humiliating reminder of just how naïve and foolish she'd been.

An expensive dress and a slick hairstyle didn't make her wife material as he'd once cruelly pointed out.

Tariq had never met her mother, which was a shame, she thought miserably, because they would have had plenty in common, most notably the belief that she didn't fit into the glittering society they both frequented.

It didn't matter, she told herself firmly as she felt a sudden rush of insecurity. She had her own life now and it was a life that she loved. A life that suited her. She'd learned to do the glossy stuff because it was expected of her, but that was only a small part of her existence.

And it wasn't the part she cared about. *Wasn't the part that she considered important.*

But that was something she had no intention of sharing with Tariq. Her brief relationship with him had taught her that being open and honest just led to pain and anguish. *And she'd learned to protect herself.*

Music poured through the open doors, indicating that the dancing had begun. Farrah knew that in half an hour the fashion show would be starting. The fashion show in which she'd been persuaded to take part. But how could she? How could she walk down that catwalk, knowing that he was in the audience?

She'd call Henry, the family chauffeur. Ask him to come and get her.

The best way to protect herself right now was to leave.

Having planned her escape, she made to step past him but he caught her arm, long strong fingers closing over her bare flesh in a silent command.

'This conversation is not finished. I have not given you permission to leave.'

She almost laughed. For Tariq, the use of power was second nature. He'd been born to command and did so readily. At the tender age of eighteen she'd been dazzled by that power. Hypnotized by his particular brand of potent sexuality. *Mesmerized by the man.*

Even now, with his hard masculine body blocking her escape, she felt the hot, hot sizzle of excitement flare inside her. *And ignored it.*

'I don't need your permission, Tariq.' Her eyes flashed a challenge and anger rose inside her. *Anger at herself for responding to a man who had hurt her.* 'I live my life the way I choose to live it and fortunately it no longer includes you. This was a chance meeting which we'd both do well to forget.'

And she *was* going to forget it, she vowed dizzily, as she struggled to control the throb of her heart and the slow, delicious curl of awareness in her stomach.

These feelings weren't real. *They weren't what mattered.*

'Do you really think that our meeting tonight has anything to do with chance?' He was standing so close to her that she could feel the heat of his body burning through the shimmering fabric of her gold dress and, even as she fought against it, she felt her limbs weaken in an instinctive feminine response to his blatant masculinity. Even though she was wearing impossibly high heels, his height and the width of his shoulders ensured that he dominated her physically. Being this close was both torment and temptation and she felt a helpless rush of wild excitement that she was powerless to quash. *And she knew, from the sudden harshness of his breathing, that he was feeling it too.*

It had always been that way between them.

From that first day at the beach.

From their first kiss at the Caves of Zatua, deep in the desert.

It was the reason why she'd made such a total fool of herself. She'd been blinded by a physical attraction so powerful and shattering that it transcended common sense and cultural differences.

For a moment she stood, frozen into stillness by the strength of his presence. There was something intensely sexual about him. Something raw and untamed. *Something primitively male.* She'd sensed it from the first moment of meeting him and she felt it again now as she stood, trapped by her own uncontrollable response to him. Her nipples hardened and thrust against the fabric of her dress and something dark and dangerous uncurled low in her stomach and spread through her body.

And then sounds of laughter from the ballroom broke the sensual spell that had stifled her ability to think and move.

With a flash of mortification, she stepped away from him and reminded herself of the lessons she'd learned in the wild desert land of Tazkash. She'd learned that a deep enduring love combined with wild, ferocious, untamed passion wasn't always enough.

She'd learned that he was ruthless and cynical and that their personalities and expectations just didn't match.

'You expect me to believe that you engineered this?' She threw her head back and laughed. 'Tariq, you were at such pains to be rid of me five years ago that I know that cannot possibly be true. I was unsuitable, remember? You were ashamed of me.'

Just as her mother had been ashamed of her.

'You were young.' His tone was cool. 'I've watched you with interest over the years.'

Her eyes widened in shock. 'Watched me?'

'Of course.' He gave a wry smile. 'You're rarely out of the press. Designers fight to have you wear their clothes on the red carpet. If you wear a dress, then it sells.'

And how sad was that? Farrah mused, producing a false smile designed to indicate that such an 'accolade' mattered to her. In truth, the thought that people regarded her—her—as a fashion icon was as ridiculous as it was laughable. Almost as laughable as the idea that Tariq had noticed and cared.

He was a man who negotiated peace settlements and billion dollar oil deals. It was hard to believe that he could be genuinely interested in something as superficial as the contents of her wardrobe, but she'd long since resigned herself to the fact that her priorities seemed to be different from those of almost everyone else on the planet. She cared about different things.

But, thanks to her mother, she'd learned to stay quiet about her real interests. Had learned to play the game she was expected to play and she played it now, lifting her chin, hiding behind the image she'd created for herself. She watched his eyes narrow as he studied her expression.

'You've developed poise, Farrah. And elegance.'

And duplicity. She was the master of pretence. Concealing her frustration behind another smile, she wondered why it was that everyone was so obsessed with how she looked on the outside. Didn't *anyone* care about the person behind the glitter? Wasn't anyone interested in who she really was?

Memories, painful and hurtful, twisted inside her.

For a short blissful time she'd thought Tariq was interested. *She'd thought he cared.* But she'd been wrong.

And his rejection had been the final spur for her to reinvent herself. To finally become the woman her mother had always wanted her to be. *At least for part of the time*. For the rest of the time she led an entirely different life. The life she wanted to lead. A life that few knew about.

A life she had absolutely no intention of sharing with Tariq.

'I'm glad you approve,' she said smoothly, stepping aside so that she could walk past him. 'And now I need to go and—'

'You're not going anywhere.' Without hesitation, he caught her round the waist and jerked her towards him. She lifted a hand in an instinctive gesture of defense, but it was too late. Her body had felt the hard brush of his thighs and responded instantly.

She shook her head to clear the clouds of dizziness and sucked in a lungful of air but even that was a mistake because the air contained the delicious, erotic scent of him and the clouds around her brain just grew denser.

Struggling to find the control that she was so proud of, she held herself rigid in his arms. 'Why would you suddenly seek me out? I can hardly believe you find yourself short of female company.'

'I'm not short of female company.'

His cool statement shouldn't have caused pain but it did and she dragged her eyes away from her involuntary study of his dark jaw.

'Then go and concentrate your attentions on someone who's interested,' she suggested, squashing down memories of past humiliation. 'I'm not. And I want you to let me go.'

The tension between them was overwhelming. 'If you're not interested,' he said silkily, 'why is your heart pounding against mine?'

Farrah decided that if there was anything worse than feeling this way, it was knowing that he was aware of her reaction. 'I don't like being held against my will,' she said frostily, a flash of anger in her eyes as she looked at him. 'And I don't like the way you use power and control to get your own way. I don't respond to bullying.'

'You think I'm bullying you?' His tone was lethally soft, his mouth only a breath away from hers. 'That's strange, because I let go of you the moment you requested that I do so, but you haven't moved an inch, Farrah. Your body is still against mine. Why is that? I wonder.'

She gave a soft gasp and stepped back, realising that he was telling the truth. He was no longer holding her.

'I think what holds us together is sexual chemistry,' he murmured, a self-satisfied look in his eyes as he lifted a hand to her flushed cheek, 'the way it always did. Which proves I was right to seek you out.'

From somewhere, she found her voice. 'Why would you do that? What possible reason could you have for seeking me out?'

A man like Tariq did nothing on impulse. His schedule was punishing. Every moment of his day was planned in minute detail. Even when they'd been together, she'd had problems getting to see him. It was extremely unlikely that he would have been at an event like this without a purpose.

Was she that purpose? And if so, why? What did she have that he could possibly want?

There was a brief silence while he studied her beneath distractingly thick dark lashes. 'Five years is a long time. You were young and impulsive. You had no knowledge of my country or culture. It was, perhaps, inevitable that there would be problems between us. Misunderstandings.'

The injustice of his remarks stung her and her spine stiffened.

She'd been young, yes. A few weeks past her eighteenth birthday. Impulsive? Probably. But she'd also been ruthlessly manipulated by those around him, *those who professed to be close to him*. She'd been well and truly flattened by palace politics.

'I don't want to talk about the past and I'm not interested in your opinion, Tariq.' Her voice was flat. 'It was a long time ago and we've both moved on.'

'I don't think so.' His eyes, dark as night, slid down her

slender frame and he reached out and lifted her right hand. 'You still wear my ring.'

The ring.

With something approaching horror her gaze slid to the sparkling dramatic stone. The ring had been the embodiment of all her girlish dreams and even when their relationship had fallen apart she hadn't been able to bring herself to take it off.

Cursing herself for being so sentimental, she snatched her hand away from his. The ring was exquisitely beautiful. A diamond so rare and perfect that she'd fallen in love with it on sight. *As she had with the man who had given it to her.* 'Actually, Tariq, I wear it to remind me that men bearing extravagant gifts are not to be trusted.'

An indulgent smile spread across his bronzed features. 'Fool yourself if you wish, *laeela*, but not me. Strong feelings are not so easily extinguished. There are some things that remain unaffected by the passage of time.'

Like pain, she thought dully.

'Just go, Tariq.' Her heart was beating frantically and the shivering started up again. 'If you want closure for what happened between us, then you have it. But go, and leave me alone to live my life.' She was fine, she told herself firmly. Really, she was absolutely fine.

'Closure. Such an American word.' He looked at her thoughtfully. 'You should not walk around in the night air, half undressed. You will catch a chill.'

Before she could anticipate his intention, he shrugged his shoulders out of his jacket and draped it around her bare shoulders.

Once again she was enveloped by the familiar masculine scent and her senses swam.

He leaned closer to her, his breath warm on her cheek. 'I did not come here to seek closure, Farrah. That is not the reason that I'm here tonight.' His voice was a soft, seductive purr and she flattened herself against the cold, hard stone of the balcony that skirted the terrace.

'Then why are you here? Can we get to the point so that I can go back into the ballroom?' He was standing too close to her. She felt stifled. Suffocated. And she didn't want to wear the jacket. It was too intimate. Too much a part of him.

But, before she could remove it, he closed in on her, the width of his shoulders ensuring that he was the focus of her gaze. She could no longer see the ballroom or the bodyguard. She could no longer see the terrace. All she could see was glittering dark eyes and a hard, sensual mouth that knew how to drive a woman to distraction. And she'd forgotten about the jacket.

'Tariq—' His name was a plea on her lips and his own mouth curved slightly in acknowledgment of that plea. He could see everything, she thought desperately. He *knew* everything. Her thoughts. Her feelings. *The strange buzz in her body*. He had access to all of it.

'As I said, there are some things that the passage of time doesn't change. It is still there between us,' he said softly, lifting a hand and brushing her cheek gently with his fingers. 'That is good.'

His touch made her nerve endings tingle and her mind flickered to the rumours that abounded. It was said that there was nothing that Tariq al-Sharma didn't know about women. That he was a skilful lover. The best.

She'd never been given the opportunity to find out.

'There is nothing between us.' From somewhere deep inside her, she found her voice. 'You killed it, Tariq.'

His smile hovered somewhere between self satisfied and amused. 'Denial is useless when the body speaks so clearly.'

'You want my body to speak clearly? Fine.' Goaded by the expression on his face, she lifted a hand and slapped him hard across the cheek. From the darkness of the terrace bodyguards surged forward but Tariq halted their progress with a smooth lift of his hand, his eyes locked on hers in incredulous disbelief.

'You believe in living dangerously, *laeela*. But I forgive your reaction because I understand the depth of feeling that inspired such a move on your part.' The brief flare of anger in his dark eyes subsided, to be replaced by something slumbrous and infinitely more dangerous. 'There was always heat between us. And, despite what you may think, I don't want a meek, submissive wife.'

Coming to terms with the realization that not only had she just hit someone for the first time her life but she'd chosen to be violent with someone who could probably have her arrested, Farrah looked at him blankly, mortified that she'd lost control and shocked by her own uncharacteristic behaviour. 'Wife? You have a wife now?'

The possibility that he'd married someone in the five years since they'd met hadn't entered her head, but of course he would have married. Even a man as commitment phobic as Tariq couldn't avoid it for ever. It was his duty. Had she not recognized the pressures on him right from the start? Someone suitable and approved of by his wretched, interfering family. Why should she care? Why would it matter to her? She should pity the girl in question.

'I don't have a wife *yet*.' His tone was silky smooth. 'But you have led the conversation round to the reason for me being here this evening.'

'You're looking for a wife?' Her tone was faintly sarcastic. 'Then step back into the ballroom, Tariq. I'm sure they'll be queuing up.'

'They probably would be—' he gave a dismissive shrug '—but there's no need for me to look because the woman I intend to marry is standing in front of me.' He inclined his dark head and his mouth hovered close to hers. 'I've decided that I want you as my wife, Farrah. I have decided to marry you.'

CHAPTER TWO

FARRAH stood in shocked silence.

I want you as my wife…I have decided to marry you.

His words spun round and round in her head and when she finally spoke her voice was little more than a whisper. 'Is this some sort of sick joke?'

Once, to marry him had been her dream. And he knew it. Was he taunting her with her naïvety?

'As you well know, I have never found the prospect of marriage even remotely amusing.' Ebony brows locked in a frown. 'Why would you accuse me of joking?'

'Because you can't possibly be serious? We've had no contact for *five* years! And on the last occasion we were together—which, by the way, was when you told me that you could *never* marry a woman like me—' she supplied helpfully, 'you informed me that I was perfect mistress material but nothing else!'

Just saying the words aloud started her shivering again. You thought you'd recovered from something, she thought to herself as she tried to control her reaction, and then you realized that it had been there all along. Buried. *Waiting to be uncovered.*

People who said that time healed were lying. You made adjustments. You learned to live with things that you couldn't change. But that didn't mean that healing had taken place.

'Actually, I was wrong. Five years ago you were too young and innocent to be perfect mistress material.' Tariq studied her thoughtfully and he lifted a hand to touch her flushed cheek. 'The perfect mistress should be sexually experienced and emotionally detached. You were neither.'

The colour in her cheeks deepened and she pulled away from him. 'I'm not interested in your definition of the perfect mistress. It was a role I rejected, if you remember.'

He gave a slow smile. 'Oh, I remember. You were holding out for a much larger prize.'

'I made the mistake of thinking that our relationship meant something.'

'It did. We were good together,' he said smoothly. 'And, had you come to my bed, you would have experienced the true meaning of the word "pleasure."'

Her body heated with an explosive flash and she dragged her eyes away from the knowing gleam in his. 'Had I come to your bed, I would have been a total idiot and would have discovered the true meaning of the word "regret."'

He inhaled sharply. 'I made you an *extremely* generous offer.'

'Generous offer? Sorry, but I don't see what's generous about inviting someone to have sex with you.' She'd *loved* him, for goodness' sake. Passionately. Deeply. To the exclusion of all others. She'd believed he'd loved her. 'You're supposed to have a brilliant brain and a razor-sharp intellect but you know absolutely *nothing* about relationships or human emotions!'

'Being my "mistress" as you so quaintly call it, would have come with significant perks.'

'So basically you were offering me money in exchange for sex.' Her voice was filled with derision. 'There's a word for that, Tariq, and it isn't nice.'

His proud head lifted and the flash of his eyes was a reminder that he wasn't accustomed to being challenged. 'A marriage was not possible between us at that time.'

'But now it is?' She couldn't keep the sarcasm out of her voice but he didn't react.

'Five years is a long time. You were very young. Much can be forgiven.'

'Maybe. But I'm not the one that needs forgiving here.' She was guilty of nothing more than being gullible and the injustice of the situation stung her deeply. She forgot he was the ruling Sultan of an oil rich state and one of the most eligible and influential men in the world. To Farrah, Tariq al-Sharma was just the man who had hurt her. She saw no further than that. Cared nothing for appearances or protocol. 'You were utterly ruthless, Tariq. When I refused your "generous offer", my father and I were forced to leave the country.'

His expression revealed nothing. 'In the circumstances, it was not appropriate for you to stay.'

She thought of the desert and the beaches. She thought of the golden temples and the dusty streets. She thought of the mysteries of the souk and she thought of those precious early morning walks on the beach, warmed by the hot, hot sun. She thought of the Caves of Zatua and the legend of Nadia and her Sultan. 'For a short time it was my home. I loved it. Leaving was hard.'

But not as hard as it had been to leave Tariq.

She'd felt as though a huge part of her had been left behind in the desert. The only part of her that mattered. She'd believed that he loved her and the discovery that his feelings had been no more than sexual had shattered her fragile self-confidence.

'If you truly loved my country then you will be only too happy to return.'

'I will never return.' For her, Tazkash was a place that would always be linked with him. A place where there were too many painful memories. 'You're being ridiculous and I refuse even to have this conversation with you. I'm not one of your subjects or even one of your adoring women.' And there were plenty of those, she thought grimly. Women prepared to do just about anything to gain his attention.

'Once, Farrah Tyndall,' he said softly, the pad of his thumb brushing over the fullness of her lower lip, 'once, you begged me to marry you. You couldn't wait to climb into my bed. It was I who slowed the pace because you were so young. Once, you adored me.'

Her heart was thumping with rhythmic force against her chest. She didn't want to be reminded of just how open and honest she'd been with him about her feelings. Most women played it cool. At the age of eighteen, in love with a staggeringly sexy man, she hadn't understood the meaning of the word. How he must have laughed at her. 'That was before I discovered that princes work better in fairy tales. Before I discovered what a cold, unfeeling bastard you are.'

His head jerked back and his dark eyes narrowed in a warning. 'Be careful. I have always allowed you more leeway than most but no one speaks to me in such a way—'

'Which just goes to show what an unsuitable wife I would make. I thought you'd already made that discovery for yourself but it's good to remind you of that fact.' She shrugged her bare shoulders out of his jacket and handed it back to him. 'Thanks, but I don't need this. I prefer to go inside to warm up.'

He couldn't be serious about marrying her. Why would he be? She didn't understand what game he was playing, but she knew she didn't want to be a part of it.

Something flickered in his eyes. Something dangerous. 'You will come with me. Now.' It was an unmistakable command and she gave a slight shiver of reaction.

No one argued with Tariq—she should have remembered that. His authority was absolute. Once, his status alone had been sufficient to render her tongue-tied, but not any more. She'd had plenty of time to reflect on what had happened between them. And she'd grown up.

'Why would I want to go anywhere with you?' She forced herself to speak lightly. Forced herself not to betray the effect he had on her. 'So that you can show me the way to paradise? I've been there once before, Tariq, and I think I must have taken a wrong turning because, frankly, it wasn't up to much. Excuse me, I'm going back inside.'

Long bronzed fingers caught her wrist in a steely grip. 'I wish to talk to you properly. In private.'

'But I don't wish to talk to you in private, or in public, come to that. Five minutes in your company has been enough to convince me that you haven't changed one bit so take my advice and quit while you're only slightly behind.'

His glance reflected barely contained frustration. 'You *will* come with me.'

'Why? Because you order it? I don't wish to go anywhere with you so what are you going to do? Kidnap me?'

His dark eyes were suddenly veiled. 'I hardly think such extreme measures will be required.'

She risked a glance at him and realized with a jolt that he was deadly serious. *He wanted her*. Why? She wondered desperately. Because she'd finally managed to reinvent herself? Because, on the surface at least, she'd turned into the woman her mother had always wanted her to be? 'Do you really think I'm going to walk back into your arms?'

'If you're honest about your feelings, then yes. It's still there. Farrah—' he used his superior strength to hold her fast when she would have run '—you can feel it and so can I. And I'm offering you what you've always wanted. Don't let a childish tantrum deprive you of your dream.'

Her heart thundered against her chest. 'Even for a sultan, you are *insufferably* arrogant,' she gasped, trying to ignore the tiny shockwaves that gripped her body. 'And any dreams I might have had about you ended five years ago. You had your chance with me, Tariq, and you blew it. End of story.'

Far from being disconcerted, his eyes gleamed and she remembered too late that Tariq thrived on challenge. He was a man who hunted for obstacles just so that he could smash them down and prove his superiority.

'I am willing to play this your way for a while, Farrah, while you get used to the idea that we are going to be together again. But as my future wife you must abide by a certain code of behaviour. I understand you are to take part in the charity fashion show imminently.'

Farrah stared at him blankly. The fashion show? She'd forgotten all about the fashion show. The only thing on her mind since he'd walked on to the terrace had been escape. *From him and from her jumbled feelings*. His reminder of her commitment to the charity made her heart drop. She wasn't at all sure she could make it through another couple of hours, especially not in such a public way. Everyone would be looking at her. *Including Tariq*.

She opened her mouth to tell him that she was going to make her excuses but his eyes flashed dark and menacing, his ebony brows drawn together in a disapproving frown.

'I forbid you to take part.'

'You forbid—?' The word made her temper simmer and suddenly she struck on a foolproof way of removing him from her life again. After all, wasn't her 'inappropriate behaviour' one of the main reasons he'd cited for being unable to marry her? 'You don't want me to be in the fashion show, Tariq?' Suddenly she realized that appearing in the fashion show would be the perfect way of guaranteeing his rapid exit from her life.

'As my future wife, it would not be appropriate.'

'Good, that settles it, then,' she said sweetly as she twisted her arm free of his grip, 'because I intend to do the fashion show. So perhaps you'd better look elsewhere for the wife you so desperately need, Your Excellency.'

He inhaled sharply, disbelief flickering in his dark eyes.

'You persist in this ridiculous pretence that you're not interested. Do you understand what it is that I am proposing?'

'Proposing?' She tilted her head and her eyes sparkled with anger. 'Sorry, I didn't actually hear a proposal. I heard you ordering and forbidding and doing all the things that you're really, *really* good at. You're going to have to go and find someone else to command, Tariq, because I'm not interested.'

Without giving him a chance to respond, she walked past his bodyguards, back through the ballroom and into the room where they were frantically preparing for the fashion show. Her heart was thumping, her hands felt clammy and she felt physically sick as she joined the other girls who were modelling that evening.

His wife?

Why would he say such a thing?

Why on earth would he suddenly be talking about marrying her after five years of silence? What was going on? And why did her body still respond even though she knew what sort of man he was?

Like all addictive habits, she thought gloomily, you always wanted what was bad for you. And Tariq was extremely bad.

'Farrah, thank goodness!' Enzo Franconi, the famous Italian designer, embraced her with relief. 'We thought you'd gone home and I have the most *spectacular* dress for you to wear tonight. I predict that you will shine, you will positively dazzle, you will—'

'No dress.' Farrah's tone was grim as she slipped off her shoes and yanked the pins out of her hair. 'Are you showing any swimwear, Enzo?' Her hair fell smooth and sleek down her back while Enzo gaped in astonishment.

'Of course. But you never model swimwear. Always you refuse to dress in anything so revealing.'

Farrah's mind was on Tariq. On his proposal of marriage.

He couldn't have been serious. It didn't make sense. 'Well, tonight I'm not refusing. I'll wear whatever you've got—but preferably the most shocking, daring thing in your collection.'

She didn't understand what the Desert Prince was doing here tonight. But there was one thing that she did know for sure. If she wore something revealing on the catwalk he wouldn't be bothering her again. A man as traditional and conservative as Tariq appreciated subtlety and dignity and she was determined to offer neither. She was going to drive him away by being as unsuitable as it was possible to be.

'I do have something—' Enzo waved a hand in a gesture as nervous as it was excited '—but you would *never* agree to wear it.'

'I'm sure it will be absolutely perfect.' *Perfect to send Tariq as far away from her as possible.* Once he had seen her making a display of herself in public he would march out of the room and she could get on with her life.

Enzo prowled around her, unable to believe his luck. 'On you—' he clapped his hands and an assistant came running to his side '—it will look sensational. I predict that men will faint.'

'Well, let's hope so,' Farrah said flatly, allowing Enzo's assistant to unzip her dress, 'and let's hope that one man in particular bangs his head hard when he hits the floor.'

'Who?' Enzo lifted a wisp of material in bright peacock blue from the rail next to him and then did a double take. 'Is that mud on your leg?'

'What?' She glanced down and blushed. 'Oh—sorry—' she scrubbed it clean with her finger and Enzo gave a soft smile.

'You have been helping those children in the riding school again—'

Farrah glanced around her nervously to see who might be listening. 'We had a little girl with cerebral palsy today,' she whispered. 'You should have seen her face when we put her on the horse, Enzo.' This man was her friend, she reminded herself, one of the few people who she could trust with the secret of her real life.

'Marvellous, *cara*.' Enzo sighed and shook his head as he watched her remove the final traces of mud. 'But did you have to bring the stables into the ballroom?'

'I was held up so I changed in the car.' Farrah gave a dismissive shrug and Enzo looked at her through narrowed eyes.

'So now tell me why you are suddenly wearing a swimming costume. It is about a man, obviously. You wish to make him jealous, no?'

'Jealous?' Staring at the costume on the hanger, she shook her head in disbelief, wondering how so little material actually attached itself to the body. 'No, I don't want to make him jealous. I want to make him run.'

She didn't want him in her life a second time.

Enzo frowned. 'Then take my advice and do not wear this costume. There is not a man alive who will run having seen you dressed in this. You will find yourself with the opposite problem.'

'You don't know this man. Give it to me.' Farrah held out a hand. 'I'll get changed behind the curtain.'

'Farrah, *tesoro*—' Enzo's tone was dry as he relinquished the garment '—if you need to get dressed behind a curtain, then that is *not* the costume for you.'

'If it serves its purpose then it will be fine.' Dressed only in her underwear, she walked in bare feet into the makeshift cubicle. 'Oh, and Enzo, ask someone to find me spectacular shoes. High heels. *Really* high heels.'

Enzo's eyes gleamed and he kissed the ends of his fingers in a gesture of approval. 'Almost, I feel sorry for this man.'

'I don't need you to feel sorry for him. I just need you to make me look shocking. I need to be unsuitable wife material.' She jerked the curtain across and her courage faltered. What the hell was she doing? Adrenaline surged through her body, fuelling her determination to go through with her plan. Before reason could take over and she could change her mind, she removed her underwear and wriggled into the costume. 'Enzo? Are you out there? This thing doesn't fit—'

The designer pulled back the curtain and sighed. 'Not like that—' He stepped forward and made several adjustments that had Farrah blushing. 'Better. Much better. And now this—' He flung a transparent filmy wrap over her shoulders and she looked at it with a frown.

'I don't want to cover up.'

'This covers nothing,' Enzo said dryly, his hands tweaking and coaxing the fabric until he was satisfied. 'It is designed to draw the eye. To tempt and tease.' He narrowed his gaze, nodded with approval and then snapped his fingers towards his assistant who was hovering at a discreet distance. 'Shoes?'

Farrah gave a wry smile as she slipped her feet into a pair of designer shoes with delicate straps and vertiginous heels. 'This is all going to be wasted if I fall off the shoes, break my neck and give myself two black eyes in the process.'

'Never.' Enzo frowned and stood back as the hairdresser took over. 'Leave it loose. Yes. Like that. She looks sensational. I predict that the costume will be this season's big seller.' He glanced at Farrah with a smile. 'You wear heels that high all the time. You will not fall.'

Farrah thought of the muddy riding boots in the back of the family limousine. 'Not all the time.'

Finally Enzo was satisfied and he stood back with a nod. 'It is perfect. You are perfect, and totally wasted in this life of yours.'

They shared a secret smile and impulsively Farrah leaned forward to give her friend a hug. 'You've helped me so much,' she whispered. 'You taught me how to dress, how to walk, how to—'

'Enough—' Enzo waved a hand to stop her but there was pleasure in his smile. 'I had good material to work with. You could be a model, *cara*.'

'No, thanks.' Farrah walked towards the entrance where the other girls were lining up and Enzo caught her arm.

'Not like that! You are walking as if you are angry and out for revenge and I taught you better than that! Your eyes spark and your mouth pouts. You look as though you're going to *kill* someone, not seduce them.'

Farrah wondered what he'd say if he knew how close to the truth he was. She was angry. *Angry and hurt*.

'This costume is about being a woman.' Enzo gave her a slow smile. 'Your eyes should say "look at me", your mouth should say "kiss me" and your walk should say—'

'Yes, all right,' Farrah interrupted him quickly. 'I think I get the message.' She sucked in a deep breath and tried to calm herself.

After all, wasn't that an even better way of displaying her anger to Tariq? For a man like him, displaying herself in such a public place would be enough to make him stalk towards the exit without a backward glance in her direction.

The music pulsed and she took her position near the entrance to the catwalk.

Tariq was in for a shock.

Still coming to terms with the fact that his first ever proposal of marriage had met with a decidedly unenthusiastic response, Tariq lounged in his seat in brooding silence, waiting for the fashion show to begin.

It was typical, he mused with growing tension, that she should refuse to turn down an opportunity to flaunt herself in public. It was one of the reasons that their relationship had floundered in the first place. He'd been able to see too much of the mother in the girl. The exact details of Sylvia Tyndall's early death had been kept out of the press, but her incessant wild partying had supported the rumours that her death had been linked with drugs or alcohol or possibly a mixture of the two.

If anything, Farrah appeared to have grown even more like her mother over the years.

His long fingers drummed a slow, steady rhythm on the table as he pondered their encounter on the terrace.

All traces of the innocent girl he'd met on the beach had gone. But why should that surprise him? The young girl who'd captivated him so completely had been nothing more than an illusion. At that particular point in his life he'd been jaded and unsettled and he'd been ensnared by her fresh, unspoiled enthusiasm for life. He'd enjoyed her sense of humour and unguarded response to him. She'd appeared to be refreshingly unaware of her own breathtaking beauty. He'd found her to be modest and even a little shy. Uninterested in material things or in glamorous social gatherings.

But events had proved him wrong on so many counts.

Everything had changed from the moment they'd moved from the desert to his palace.

Gone had been the respectable mode of dress and the caring attitude. In its place a woman who'd appeared to care for nothing except her appearance. A woman who'd gone to enormous efforts to shock those around her. A woman who'd wanted to do nothing but party.

In a sense that had made her easier to deal with because he'd been dealing with women like her for almost all of his life. Women who played games. Women who traded beauty for other, more tangible, benefits, from extravagant gifts to an excellent marriage.

He skimmed a glance over the women who were now strutting down the catwalk, but only to ensure that none of them was Farrah.

He knew her well enough to realize that his request that she abandon the fashion show would be met by defiance but, even so, her entrance, made even more dramatic by the use of spotlights and pumping rock music, took him by surprise.

Her golden hair flowed long and loose over her shoulders

and was the only thing that kept the dramatic swimming costume even vaguely decent.

There was a collective murmur of appreciation from the men in the room and by his side Hasim Akbar made a strangled sound. In contrast, Tariq sat still, the flicker of a muscle in his cheek the only indication of his soaring stress levels.

The music pounded in a hypnotic rhythm that was unashamedly sexual and she started to walk in time to the beat, her movements graceful and seductive. It shouldn't have been possible to walk on the heels she was wearing but she made it look natural, as if she'd been born with high, slender spikes attached to her feet.

The swimsuit was cleverly cut to expose her long, long legs, her narrow waist and the tempting thrust of her breasts. A diaphanous wrap floated around her body, giving the illusion that she was walking through mist.

She was a vision of feminine perfection, every man's fantasy, and Tariq felt sharp claws of lust drag through his loins.

A temporary marriage came with definite benefits, he conceded. Not only would he gain ownership of the shares that were crucial for the future of his country, but he would have Farrah Tyndall naked and at his disposal for forty days and forty nights. As newly-weds he could justifiably keep her trapped in his bed and then he would divorce her before she had the opportunity to embarrass him the way she was embarrassing him now.

On the opposite side of the catwalk a man half rose to his feet, a look of naked longing in his eyes.

Devoured by ever increasing tension, Tariq discovered a hitherto untapped possessive streak deep within himself.

She was inviting male attention, he thought grimly, and she was doing it to taunt him. It was clear to him that she was still sulking over his rejection five years previously.

He lounged in his chair, simmering with ever increasing

anger as he watched what he perceived to be a deliberate attempt to provoke him.

But, instead of making him stride from the room, her intentionally provocative display merely served to reconcile him finally to the concept of marriage.

He was determined to make her his.

He should have done it five years ago, he mused in brooding silence, but instead he'd respected her innocence. He'd valued her purity. Had taken his time, the better to savour the moment when he would finally make her his.

Clearly his restraint had been wasted since she appeared to place no such value on herself.

She reached the end of the catwalk, dropped a hip in a pose deliberately designed to inflame and finally she directed her gaze in his direction. Green eyes locked on his in blatant challenge.

Try and stop me, her gaze said, and Tariq rose to his feet in a fluid movement, determined to do exactly that.

Anger roared inside him like a wild, untamed beast and he stepped onto the catwalk, ignoring the astonished scramble of his security team as they attempted to intercept him.

Without uttering a word, he swung her into his arms and strode out of the ballroom without glancing left or right. He was boiling and angry and he realized that he hadn't known the true meaning of the word *possessive* until that moment.

'Tariq—' Her voice was a shocked breathless pant as she pushed at his shoulders. 'What are you doing?'

Her words irritated him because they drew attention to the fact that for the first time in his life he'd acted without thought. *He didn't know what he was doing.* His actions had nothing to do with reason and everything to do with some dark, primitive need to remove her from the line of sight of every man in the room. If it had been within his power, he would have removed her from their minds and fantasies too, but the man in him knew that it was already too late for that. She'd ensured herself a place in every erotic dream.

The thought made him tighten his grip in raw, naked jealousy and she wriggled.

'Put me down!'

He was sorely tempted to do just that. Every part of him that mattered was in contact with smooth, warm female flesh—female flesh that squirmed in protest against certain vital parts of his body. Something dark and primitive broke loose and anger flared inside him.

Anger at her for deliberately provoking him.

Anger at himself for responding in such a predictable fashion.

Always, in her company, he found himself facing parts of himself that he didn't want to acknowledge, Tariq thought with grim honesty.

'You chose to invite attention, *laeela*—' he tried to ignore the low, throbbing ache that threatened to test his legendary self-control '—and now you have it.' He strode through the opulent foyer, through revolving doors and out to the street where his car awaited his return.

She weighed virtually nothing, he thought, as he all but thrust her into the car and delivered instructions to his driver in a clipped, angry tone.

'Tariq, I'm not going with you—'

'Be silent!' Still seething, he shrugged out of his jacket for the second time that evening and dropped it into her lap. 'Put this on.'

'I don't—'

'Cover yourself!' The ferocity of his tone shocked even him so he could hardly blame her for shrinking back in her seat. Her reaction shamed him because whatever his faults, he had never struck a woman and never would. He was a man who prided himself on his self-control and yet at that precise moment he wanted to kill someone. 'You are barely dressed,' he said flatly, turning his head so that he didn't have to look at the confusion in her eyes. He didn't want to feel sympathy. *Didn't want to feel anything*. 'When we reach my home, my staff will find you something more suitable to wear.'

Preferably something that covered every inch of her.

She glared at him. 'You're behaving like a caveman.'

'If I were a caveman then I would have followed my baser instincts and stripped you naked in the ballroom when you all but begged me to do so,' he said silkily, 'and you would now be lying naked on one of those tables and your pleasure would be so great that you would be sobbing and begging for mercy.'

Her soft gasp of shock was at odds with her provocative appearance. 'I would never beg you for anything,' she said hoarsely, but her gaze held his for a fraction longer than necessary and his gaze hardened.

Experience told him that she was clearly not indifferent to him, no matter how much she would have liked that to be the case.

The attraction between them was as strong as ever and he was willing to overlook her less appealing traits in order to have her naked in his bed.

The marriage might be short lived, Tariq mused silently, but sexually it promised to be full-on and immensely satisfying.

'I don't want to go anywhere with you. Just drop me home, please.' Her tone was flat but she slipped her arms into the jacket and closed it around her. She was so slender that it would have been possible to fit two of her inside but she was also tall and the jacket did nothing to conceal the tempting length of her legs. Clearly aware of that fact, she pressed her knees together and slid her legs closer to the seat.

Tariq gave a predatory smile. 'It's a little late for modesty, don't you think?' For some reason the sight of her bare, beautiful legs served to reignite the anger that he'd only just managed to subdue. 'Charity balls have certainly taken an interesting turn since I was last in England. Is it suddenly a necessary requirement for the guests to reveal all?'

She didn't glance in his direction. 'It was all in a good cause.'

'If you're trying to persuade me that you really care about the charity then you're wasting your time. We both know that you just seize on any excuse to dress up and flaunt yourself in public.'

Like mother like daughter.

'That's right.' She turned her head towards him, her amazing green eyes glittering in the semi-darkness, her blond hair falling sleek and smooth over his jacket. 'I spend all day lying in bed resting so that I have enough energy to get myself through another night of drink-fuelled partying. Isn't that right, Tariq? Isn't that the person I am?'

She looked so innocent, he mused as his eyes rested on the tempting curve of her soft mouth. Nothing like a woman who'd turned flirting into an art form or a woman who was only interested in expanding the contents of her already bulging wardrobe.

'Don't try and provoke me,' he warned softly. 'Next time you wish to support a cause then let me know and I will write them a large cheque. It will save you the bother of stripping off.'

'I'll do as I please.' She lifted her chin and glared at him. 'Life is all about money to you, isn't it? All about power and influence. Well, I don't need your money and your power doesn't interest me. I don't need *anything* at all from you. The way I act, the way I behave, is nothing to do with you. You don't know me and you never did.' The words were thrown at him with careless indifference but he sensed the growing tension in her, saw her amazing green eyes darken as something live and dangerous snapped taut between them.

The car sped through the night, smooth and silent, the darkness of the interior ensuring their privacy and increasing the intimacy.

Suddenly stifled by it, Tariq lifted a hand and tugged at his tie, opening the top two buttons of his shirt with a deft movement of his lean, strong fingers. She followed the movement with her gaze, caught his eye for a single tense moment and then looked away. The silken fall of her hair concealed her face but only after he'd seen the colour pour into her cheeks.

The atmosphere was pulled tight with a sexual tension so powerful that the air throbbed and hummed.

And he knew she felt it too because he saw the rapid movement of her slender throat as she swallowed, saw her fingers clutch his jacket around her like a shield. In a self-conscious gesture she tried to tuck her legs away but there was nowhere to put them. Nowhere to hide.

'*Stop* looking at me, Tariq.' Her hoarse plea brought a faint smile to his lips and dampened some of the anger inside him.

Her almost childish plea confirmed his belief that she was suffering as much as he was. Evidently she wasn't as indifferent as she chose to appear.

'That outfit is an invitation to a man to look. It was designed entirely for that purpose,' he said smoothly, allowing his eyes to roam freely over her bare legs. 'Presumably you knew that when you chose to wear it.'

Her knuckles whitened as she clenched her hands in her lap. 'I wore it to annoy you!'

He gave a slow smile. 'Then you don't know much about men, *laeela*. In public, such an outfit would indeed annoy me but now we are in private my feelings are entirely different.'

'I'm not interested in your feelings.'

'No? We never found out, did we, *laeela*?' He leaned towards her and gently brushed her hair away from her face, revealing her exquisite profile. 'We never found out how we would be together. We dreamed and we danced around the edges of passion—those stolen meetings on the beach, kissing in the Caves of Zatua—all that foreplay—' His gaze dropped to her lips and lingered there. 'Five years. I have waited for five years to have that question answered.'

She turned her head then, her breathing rapid. 'Then I hope you're a patient man because you're going to be waiting for the rest of your life and still you won't find out. I'm not one of your toys, Tariq. I'm not yours to command. I'm not a fancy car you can buy or a jet you can fly. You can't just decide to have me.'

'Yes, I can. I have only to touch you and you will be mine.' He wound a strand of hair around his finger. 'And you want that every bit as much as I do.'

Her eyes stared into his, hypnotized. 'Not true,' she croaked. 'I don't want that. And your ego is sickening.'

'A ruler with no confidence in himself does not inspire the loyalty and devotion of his people,' he said huskily, moving his body closer to hers, 'and we both know that my ego is not the problem here. Your feelings are the problem. Or rather, your insistence on denying them. Despite what you say to the contrary, you're mentally undressing me and you're wondering how our bodies will move together when we're finally in bed. You're wondering how it will feel when I'm inside you.'

He watched the movement of her slender throat as she swallowed, saw the flash of shock in her eyes, the hint of excitement in those green depths. 'Stop it.' Her voice was a tortured whisper. 'I want you to stop it, now.'

His eyes gleamed dark with amusement. 'Do you think I was unaware of your feelings? At eighteen your sexual curiosity was hard to conceal. You hadn't learned to play games, *laeela*. Your eyes followed me everywhere and when I came near you, you felt an excitement so intense that you ceased to breathe.'

She blushed again. 'You are *so* arrogant.'

'I am honest.' He sat back in his seat, more than satisfied with her response. 'Which is more than you are. Five years ago I met the girl. Now I am eager to discover the woman. And this time we will not be flirting on the edge of passion, *laeela*, but plunging hard into its fiery depths.'

She really was astonishingly beautiful, he mused as he watched confusion flicker over her heart-shaped face as she registered his sexually explicit analogy. The prospect of marriage was growing more appealing by the minute. He was even starting to wonder whether forty days and forty nights would be long enough.

'I won't go with you, Tariq.'

'I hate to point out the obvious,' he said with gentle emphasis, 'but you *are* with me.'

'A mistake that I intend to rectify immediately.' She glanced out of the window and her eyes widened. She turned her head for an explanation, panic in her eyes. 'The airport? What are we doing at the airport?'

'As I said, I am taking you home. My home. We are going to Tazkash.' He leaned forward to speak to his driver and then turned back towards the woman who was trying to open the car door. 'Enough of playing games. I'm going to make you my wife, Farrah. And then I'm going to take you to my bed and keep you there for as long as it suits me.'

CHAPTER THREE

FARRAH sat in one of the soft leather seats inside his private jet, her slim body tense with panic as she struggled to find a way out of the current situation. She ignored the staff who discreetly provided for her every need and ignored Tariq who sprawled, relaxed and infuriatingly calm, in the seat next to her.

She was just *so* angry with him. He was high-handed, controlling, dictatorial— Her brain thumping with anger, she ran out of adjectives before she could compile a decent list.

But most of all she was furious with herself. *How* could she have got herself into this position?

How could she have forgotten what he was like?

He was arrogant and autocratic and used to dictating his desires to an audience of followers whose only purpose in life was to do his bidding.

It had been foolish of her to provoke him, she knew that now.

When he'd half flung her into the back of his limousine, she'd been so angry and churned up inside that all her emotions had been focused on him, rather than the situation. She'd given no thought whatsoever to where they were going.

When he'd said that he intended to take her to his home, she should have realized that he meant Tazkash. She should have remembered that he never played games and should have been instantly on the alert. When he'd said he intended to take her somewhere private to talk, she should have made her excuses and run, hidden.

Not taunted him.

Would she have climbed into a cage with a tiger and poked him with a stick? No, of course she wouldn't! And yet she'd as good as done exactly that with Tariq.

The more she told him that she wasn't interested, the more he seemed determined to make her his.

Why hadn't she remembered that no one ever won in a fight against the Desert Prince? How could they when he had so many weapons at his disposal? A sharp brain—astonishing mental agility had been her father's observation—and exceptional diplomatic skills. And if all else failed he had only to resort to power. He just gave an order and it was done. Instantly. Without question.

Which was how she now found herself sitting in his plane, forced to do his bidding.

She'd been so astonished to discover that their journey had taken them to the airport, so distracted by the growing tension between them, that she'd been urged up the steps and on to his waiting jet before she'd had time to formulate an escape plan.

The humiliation of walking on to the plane half naked had been intensified by the total absence of reaction on the part of his staff. It was obvious that they were accustomed to seeing Tariq arrive with a virtually naked woman in tow.

For some reason she couldn't identify, the knowledge infuriated her.

As did the way they'd bowed low and shown her into a spacious dressing room filled with a selection of clothes. They'd indicated that they were expected to help her to dress but she'd been stared at by enough people to last her a lifetime and rejected assistance in favour of privacy.

Clearly Tariq made a habit of transporting half-naked females, she'd thought angrily as she'd rummaged through the rails and settled on a silk trouser suit. It was high at the neck and long in the leg and, after the way he'd been looking at her in the car, that was all that mattered to her.

And now she was sitting next to him again, this time with a thin covering of silk to protect her legs from his masculine and blatantly sexual appraisal. It was dark outside and the dim lights of the cabin created an atmosphere of intimacy that made her thoroughly on edge.

She'd never wanted to see Tariq again.

And yet here she was. Closeted with him in the stifling intimacy of his private jet. Could anything be worse?

'Take me home, Tariq.' She turned her head to look at him, her voice cold. 'Take me home now.'

'I'm taking you to Tazkash. Your new home.'

'You can't just suddenly decide to marry someone.'

His smile was infuriatingly patient. 'Unlike some people, I don't have a problem with decision-making. I know what I want. Indecisiveness is not a trait that I value in others and even less so in myself.'

She tried another tack. 'My father will never allow it.'

'Your father is heavily involved in a project in Siberia and is currently out of contact,' he said smoothly. 'I understand that the project is extremely complex and taking all of his time. You are not currently his priority.'

She swallowed. Did he know everything? 'I can always reach my father.'

'And say what?' Tariq accepted two glasses from a stewardess and handed one to Farrah. 'That you are marrying me? He knows how much you wanted me. He would probably offer his congratulations.'

Farrah swallowed. 'You think you're such a matrimonial prize, don't you?'

Tariq smiled. 'I see the facts as they are. Dissembling and false modesty are a waste of time and not part of my nature.'

'Has it occurred to you that I don't want to marry you?'

'Why would it? Once, you could think of nothing else. Do you remember that first day that we met?' His voice was low and seductive. 'On the beach with the sun rising on the dunes behind us?'

She stared at him for a long moment and then turned her head away.

Oh, yes, she remembered.

It had been on that very first morning in Nazaar, the desert camp situated on the edge of the desert, bordered by sand and sea.

Her father had flown out to negotiate the terms of a major deal and she'd accompanied him. She'd been eighteen years old, still grieving for her mother, who had died six months previously, and still trying to be the daughter that her parents had always wanted.

She'd been walking on the beach, keen to explore her new home…

'You are an early riser, Miss Tyndall.'

The deep male voice came from directly behind her and she turned from her dreamy contemplation of the red gold dunes that rose upwards to hundreds of feet. Here, at Nazaar, the sea washed right up to the dunes, licking the edges of a desert that stretched far into the distance. It was a place designed for fantasy and dreaming, as was the man standing facing her. He stood well over six feet, his shoulders broad and muscular, his arms folded across his chest as he surveyed her with a masculine assurance that brought a soft gasp of awareness to her lips.

The subtle lift of an eyebrow was sufficient to tell her that her reaction had not gone unnoticed and she cursed herself for being so obvious. Any woman would have done the same, she told herself, struggling not to drool at the sight of the man watching her. Especially a woman who curled up in bed at night, dreaming of romance.

He was darkly exotic and staggeringly good-looking. From the proud angle of his nose and jaw to the fierce flash of his eyes, he was a man very much at home in the harshness of his surroundings. He was dressed in traditional robes, but they failed to conceal the athletic power of his physique or the width of his shoulders and the way he held himself suggested a confidence and sophistication that went far beyond that of a simple man of the desert.

An unfamiliar emotion sprang to life inside her and began to sizzle and burn.

Fear? Excitement? Perhaps a mixture of both—certainly this man was unlike any she'd met before.

An ebony brow lifted and he folded his arms across his chest, a glint of amusement in his dark eyes as he responded to her scrutiny. 'It is rude to stare, Miss Tyndall.'

'How do you know my name?' His gaze was disturbingly intent and she felt suddenly breathless and ridiculously self-conscious. 'I suppose a Western woman staying in Nazaar is unlikely to go unnoticed.' It was a place of business, her father had told her that. And in the oil rich state of Tazkash, business was the responsibility of men. Especially when it was royal business.

The hint of a smile touched his hard mouth. 'I think you are unlikely to go unnoticed in any part of the world, Miss Tyndall.'

It wasn't the compliment that made her skin prickle as much as the frankly sexual appraisal she read in the depths of those dark, dark eyes.

It wasn't the first time a man had shown interest in her, but it was the first time anyone had done so in such a blatant manner. Obviously his ego was well developed, she thought weakly as the wind picked up a strand of her hair and flung it across her face. She lifted a hand to anchor it behind her ear and discovered that she was shaking.

Still his gaze didn't waver. It was as if…as if he were making a decision about something. And she had the oddest feeling that the decision involved her in some way.

No, that was ridiculous.

Following her own preference, she was respectably and discreetly dressed but there was something about the look in his eyes that made her feel naked. Exposed. Vulnerable.

'So I'm not the only one who enjoys the beach early in the morning.' To disguise how unsettled she felt, she waved a hand and gave him a bright smile. 'It's fabulous here, isn't it? I can't believe that the sea meets the desert like this—it's like one giant beach—' She could hear herself chattering and cut herself off. She always talked too much when she was nervous. And the more she talked, the more likely she was to say the wrong thing.

His gaze didn't shift from her face. 'You like our country, Miss Tyndall?'

'Well, I haven't seen much of it,' she confided regretfully. 'My father is always too busy to accompany me. He spends the entire day in meetings with the Desert Prince.'

Something flickered in those dark, exotic eyes. 'You have met the Prince?'

'No. But that's probably just as well.' She gave a little shrug. 'I wouldn't know what to say to a prince. My father's afraid I'd say the wrong thing at the wrong time and cause offence. It's my special gift. I don't want to blow his deal out of the water so I'm keeping my head down and my mouth shut and restricting my explorations to a few walks on the beach.'

'That sounds tediously boring.' There was amusement in his dark gaze. 'Perhaps the Prince would find it refreshing to be with a woman who speaks her mind.'

'Don't count on it,' Farrah said gloomily. 'My father always says it's my biggest failing. My mouth moves before my brain. I'm trying to learn to do it the other way round, but so far it's not working. Mental and verbal coordination aren't really my thing.'

He threw his head back and laughed. It was a rich masculine sound. 'Are you interested in seeing more of our country, Miss Tyndall?'

'Of course. But it isn't that simple, unfortunately.'

'Why not?'

She frowned slightly. 'Well, I can't just take off into the desert on my own.'

'I agree that to go alone would be foolhardy, but with company it would be a different matter.'

She stared at him. 'Is that possible?'

He angled his proud head as if the question were superfluous. 'Of course. Anything can be arranged if the desire is there. Is there anything in particular you wish to see?' His voice was deep and smooth and she wondered where he'd learned to speak such perfect English.

'I want to visit the Byzantine fort at Giga, but mostly—' she turned and looked out across the desert, her expression dreamy '—mostly I want to see the Caves of Zatua.'

She wanted to see the place where Nadia was said to have met her love.

'You are familiar with the legend of Zatua?'

Of course she was familiar with the legend. She preferred it to any fairy story she'd ever heard because it was so passionate, so heartbreaking and so *real*. She'd positively *ached* for Nadia and wanted to strangle the Sultan for his foolishness.

Thinking of it now, she stared at the rich, exotic colour of the dunes. She could imagine it all so clearly. 'A local girl fell madly in love with a man only to discover that he was actually the Sultan, who had been spending time incognito among her tribe. He loved her too, but her status was so far beneath his that they were forced to keep their relationship secret. So they met in the Caves of Zatua.' She turned back to him, her green eyes misty with emotion as she retold the story that had captivated her for so long. 'Then their meetings were discovered. The Sultan wasn't prepared to challenge the expectations of his people and marry her, so he ended the relationship. She was so devastated that she killed herself rather than be with another man.'

There was amusement in his dark gaze. 'I think the legend has been modified slightly over the years,' he said dryly. 'It would have been a fairly simple act on the part of the Sultan to have the girl brought into the Harem. I see no compelling reason why the relationship had to be played out in a dark cave. And no reason at all for her to end her life when she could have been his favourite. But the tourists like the story. It has a certain tragic romance about it that they find attractive.'

Farrah frowned at his dismissive tone. 'But Nadia loved him. She didn't want to be just his mistress. She wanted to be his wife. Perhaps she refused to enter the Harem.'

'To be the Sultan's mistress would have been considered a great honour,' he said smoothly, his eyes fixed on her face, 'and one which no woman would ever wish to turn down.'

'Good enough for bed but not to wed? Well, I don't think it's that big an honour! I mean the Harem is just about sex, isn't it, and—' Realizing what she'd said, she broke off and blushed, disturbed by the indulgent humour she saw in his gaze. 'All right, so maybe I'm getting a little carried away—'

'I am beginning to understand your father's concerns. Your mouth definitely moved before your brain on that occasion, Miss Tyndall.'

She chewed her lip and brushed her hair away from her face. 'It's just that I can't actually see the honour in just climbing into bed with someone until they get tired of you.' Was he shocked? He didn't look shocked, she thought. Just amused and perhaps a little thoughtful. 'Why would you do that if you were in love? It's insulting. A woman wants so much more than that.'

'He was the Sultan.' He lifted his dark head, the gesture both arrogant and dominant. 'He could never have married a woman whose status in life was so far beneath his. It would not have been possible. She would not have been suitable.'

'If they were in love then it shouldn't have mattered,' she said passionately, '*Nothing* should have mattered. He should have thrown away his kingdom for her if that was what it took for them to be together!'

'And what about his responsibility to his people?'

'Surely they would have wanted their Sultan to be happy?'

He stared at her for a long moment, the expression in his dark eyes veiled by thick, dark lashes. 'You make it sound very simple, Miss Tyndall.'

She flushed. 'It *should* have been simple. If he'd truly loved her, then he would have done anything to be with her.'

There was a long silence and then his eyes narrowed. 'How old are you?'

She stiffened, aware that she'd said far, far too much. 'I was eighteen last week, actually. But I don't see what that has to do with anything.' Should she apologize? Should she—

'You are very young and you have a naïve, romantic view of life. And of love.' He studied her at length and gave a smile and the unexpected charm of that smile made her heart leap into her throat. 'Let's hope you are never given cause to rethink your idealistic view of the world, Miss Tyndall.'

'Do you work with the prince? Do you know him well?'

There was an ironic gleam in his eyes. 'Well enough.'

And suddenly she knew who he was and closed her eyes in mortification. 'Oh, no—'

'You can stop worrying,' he said smoothly. 'Despite what you are thinking, you said nothing to embarrass either yourself or your father. I found your frankness unusually refreshing.'

Farrah stood still, feeling hideously self-conscious and more socially inept than usual. Since her mother's death she'd struggled to be more at ease in social situations, but she'd had no experience with royalty and suddenly she felt tongue-tied. 'You're here to negotiate the pipeline deal with my father,' she muttered as she searched for something meaningful to say. 'Your father, the Sultan, doesn't want the pipeline to be built.

He wants things to stay as they've always been but the country needs to develop more wealth.'

'You appear to be an expert on the politics of Tazkash.'

Farrah bit her lip and remembered too late her mother's irritation whenever she'd overheard her talking about what she called 'serious subjects.'

Trying to redeem herself, she gave a vague smile. 'It would certainly be nice to see more of the scenery while I'm here,' she muttered, deliberately playing down her keen interest in history and architecture.

There was a brief pause. 'I would be honoured to act as your escort, Miss Tyndall,' he said gravely. 'It will be arranged.'

And just like that, it was.

A maid came to her tent just before dawn on the following morning and presented her with suitable clothing. Then she was escorted to a four-wheel drive vehicle.

Lounging in the driver's seat was the man she'd met on the beach. Only this time he was dressed casually in jeans and an open-necked shirt.

He greeted her with a smile and a faint bow of his glossy, dark head. 'Miss Tyndall. I trust you slept well.'

Actually she hadn't slept much at all and what little sleep she'd had, had been haunted by dreams of Nadia and her Sultan. For some reason the dream had been disturbingly explicit.

Pushing the memory aside, she climbed in next to him. 'Is it just the two of us? You're driving me yourself?'

'Why not?'

'I presumed a prince would be surrounded by bodyguards.'

His gaze lingered on hers for a moment and then he shifted the vehicle into gear and drove towards the road that led directly into the desert. 'Occasionally that is necessary, of course, but not for this trip. It is a two hour drive to the Fortress at Giga. We will have breakfast when we get there.'

She turned to him, excited at the prospect of visiting such a historic site, forgetting her resolve to be careful what she said. 'You give a lot of orders, don't you? A bit like my Dad. He suffers from a controlling personality too. I'm always telling him off for giving commands instead of making requests.'

'If business was conducted through a series of requests, not much would be achieved.'

'That's rubbish.' She frowned as she fastened her seat belt. 'Everyone knows that you get more from people if they buy into an idea. Giving orders simply turns people off.'

'Am I turning you off, Miss Tyndall?'

Something in his silky tone made her heart skip and dance and she resisted the urge to gulp loudly. 'I—you—I'm very pleased you're showing me round,' she finished weakly and he gave a slow smile.

'I'll try and remember to request rather than command and you need to keep that mouth of yours from misbehaving.' His gaze dropped from her eyes to her lips and she felt an almost agonizing pull deep inside her.

'I don't even know what to call you. Your Highness?'

His gaze lingered on her mouth and then he turned his attention back to the road. 'You can call me Tariq.'

And so her life changed.

Every morning she dressed quickly and hurried outside and into the four-wheel drive, eager to discover where he was taking her that day.

But by the end of the first week she'd stopped dreaming about Nadia and her Sultan and her nights were filled with hot, disturbingly erotic dreams about her own man from the desert. Tariq.

By the end of the month, she was in love.

They talked about everything and she forgot that she was trying to learn not to be so frank. Under that compelling dark gaze she revealed everything that she thought and felt. *Revealed everything about the person she was*.

And then, finally, he took her to the Caves of Zatua.

'It is a strange place to conduct a love affair, is it not?' His voice was husky in the semi-darkness as he led her deeper and deeper into the caves. 'One would imagine that they could have found somewhere more conducive to romance.'

'I think it's terribly romantic.' She stared up at the jagged rock and tried to imagine how Nadia must have felt. 'And it was the only place she could be with her Sultan without the people knowing.'

His dark eyes glittered with amusement. 'You have taken our legend to your heart, it would seem.'

'It's a sad story—' She stopped and looked around her, listening to the strange noises that were part of the cave. 'I wonder if she was ever scared? Waiting for her lover in this dark, empty place—'

'Are you scared, Miss Tyndall?' His voice was velvety smooth and she gave a shiver, aware of his powerful body close to hers.

'No.'

'Then why are you shaking?' His hand found hers in the semi-darkness and she swallowed nervously, although whether that was from the effects of her surroundings or the touch of his hand on hers, she wasn't sure. 'Do people ever get lost in here?'

'I don't know.' His smile flashed, teasing and dangerous. 'We could search for bodies if you like and then we will know.'

'Very funny, I'm sure.' The confined space and diffused light created an intimacy that was almost stifling in its intensity. She was aware of his strong grip on her hand, of the frantic beating of her heart and the dryness of her mouth. 'Do you think this is where they met?'

'Possibly. Can you imagine Nadia entwined in the arms of her Sultan?'

The image exploded in her brain with frightening clarity and she swallowed and stared at the dusty floor of the cave. *Oh, yes, she could imagine that.* 'You think it was here—?'

'Deep in the caves was the only place they could be assured

of the privacy they needed. Here, they were totally alone.' His voice was a low seductive purr and she suddenly discovered that she'd stopped breathing. 'Here they were no longer a Sultan and his mistress, but a man and a woman.'

She swallowed. 'Nadia should have known that the Sultan would reject her.'

'He didn't reject her.' His mouth was close to her ear, his breath warm on her cheek. 'He offered her the role of his mistress.'

She couldn't breathe. 'It was an insult. True love deserves a better outlet than hot sex.'

'And yet the power of hot sex is not to be underestimated, would you not agree, Farrah?' He turned her to face him, his hands hard and demanding on her shoulders. 'The feelings between a man and a woman are sometimes so powerful that they transcend common sense. Those feelings become the only thing that matter.'

She stared up at him, his dark, compelling gaze holding her captive. Shocked by the intensity of feelings that washed through her body, she felt suddenly dizzy and disorientated.

His mouth hovered tantalizingly close to hers and something hot and delicious uncurled low in her stomach. A frantic, breathless anticipation exploded inside her and her pulse started to race.

'Tariq—' She breathed his name and closed her eyes. She thought she heard him mutter, '*So be it*,' but she couldn't be certain because his mouth finally claimed hers and she lost the ability to think.

It was the kiss of her dreams.

His mouth was hot and demanding, the lean power of his body pressing against hers as he hauled her hard against him. She felt a tug at the back of her head and realized that he'd released her hair from the clip she'd used to restrain it.

He muttered something that she didn't understand and then sank his hands into her hair and held her head still while he explored her mouth in sensual, erotic detail. His fingers trailed lightly down her neck and then lower still, brushing lazily against the frantic jut of her nipple.

Desire stabbed through her, sharp and urgent, and still his mouth seduced hers, commanding her response. And she gave what he demanded. The world outside ceased to exist. She was cocooned in the heat of her own newly awakened desire, ready to give him everything. *All that she had and all that she was*.

Was this how Nadia had felt with her Sultan? She wondered dizzily.

Was this why she'd chosen death rather than a life without him?

Overwhelmed by emotion, she slid her arms round his neck. 'I love you.' She muttered the words against his clever, skilful mouth. 'This has been the best month of my life.'

He tensed and slowly lifted his head, his dark eyes scanning her face. 'You are very young, *laeela*, and extremely beautiful,' he said softly, lifting a hand and stroking his fingers through her hair, his expression thoughtful. 'You please me.'

Farrah tried to hide her disappointment. *You please me* wasn't exactly the same as *I love you*, but at least it was a start.

A shout from the entrance of the caves caught his attention. His wide shoulders stiffened with tension and there was a flash of annoyance in his dark eyes. 'Unfortunately it appears that we must return to Nazaar.' He turned back to her, his voice husky and intensely masculine. 'It is growing late and my presence is required elsewhere.'

'So? Can't you do your command thing and tell them all to go away?' She snuggled against him, wishing they could stay in the cave for ever.

There was a glimmer of humour in his gaze. 'Unfortunately not. There is a time for business and a time for pleasure. It is necessary to return now.'

She caught his arm. 'But will I see you again? What—'

'Trust me, *laeela.*' He touched a finger to her mouth. 'We will be together, that I promise you. And the pleasure will be all the greater for the wait.'

She didn't want to wait, but clearly she had no choice and she consoled herself with the fact that he obviously felt the same way that she did. He wanted them to be together.

He loved her too.

She dreamed all the way back to the desert camp and she was still dreaming when her father came to find her for dinner.

'I can't believe you didn't tell me, Farrah!' He glared at her and she struggled to concentrate on what he was saying.

'Tell you what?'

'That you have been spending every day with the Prince. Did you not think it worth mentioning?'

She hadn't mentioned it because she was afraid that her father might try and stop her.

'Prince Tariq bin Omar al-Sharma is totally out of your league,' her father said with a frown. 'You're not his type.'

Insecurity stabbed her but she ignored it. Her father hadn't been with them, she consoled herself. He hadn't seen what they'd shared. 'I love him. And he loves me, I *know* he does.'

'You're being naïve. Prince Tariq is the most eligible guy in the world. Women drop into his path.'

'And you're wondering what he could possibly see in me, aren't you?'

'The woman who finally captures the heart of the Desert Prince will be sophisticated and beautiful,' her father said wearily. 'I love you, Farrah. Just as you are. We both know that your mother tried to make you into something that you're not and you changed a lot about yourself in order to please her. But she's gone now. You can be who you really are.'

Farrah's eyes filled. 'Daddy—'

Her father shook his head, his eyes tired and empty. 'The shallow social scene isn't your thing, Farrah. And perhaps that's a good thing. It corrupted your mother. I'd hate to see it corrupt you too.'

'I'm not going to be corrupted and it isn't Tariq's thing either,' Farrah said urgently. Suddenly she needed her father to understand, needed him to give her hope. 'Tariq is interested in history and culture and things that matter.'

'He's the Crown Prince,' her father said dryly. 'He entertains world leaders. That matters too.'

Farrah thought of the month they'd spent together. Thought of their conversations, of the confidences they'd shared. 'I know he loves me.'

'Then you're a fool,' her father said quietly.

And her father had been right, Farrah thought numbly as she stared out of the window of the jet.

She *had* been a fool.

For a short, blissful, deluded time she'd managed to convince herself that Tariq loved her—*that he was going to ask her to marry him*. But marriage had never been on his mind.

Just like the Sultan and Nadia, he'd wanted their relationship to be kept a secret.

She was good enough to be his mistress, but not his wife.

The tender moments they'd spent together in the desert camp of Nazaar had been nothing more than a sophisticated seduction technique on his part. And at the age of eighteen, her brain full of romance and dreams, she'd fallen for it.

How naïve could a girl be?

But she knew better now, she reminded herself as she pressed herself back in her seat in an attempt to get as far away from him as possible.

She knew exactly what sort of man Tariq was and what sort of qualities he valued.

Obviously he'd studied her new sleek celebrity status and had decided that she was finally good enough to stand by his side. Ironically, she'd developed that side of herself in response to her mother's expectations and Tariq's own cruel rejection of her years earlier.

But only she knew that inside she hadn't changed at all. She was still the girl who preferred history and horses to house parties and hairdressers. But she had no intention of revealing herself to Tariq.

And, this time, she wasn't going to be blinded by the overwhelming sexual attraction that existed between them. No matter what the reaction of her body, she had no intention of making a fool of herself over him for a second time.

And no intention of letting him through the glittering web of deceit she'd spun to protect herself.

CHAPTER FOUR

THEY landed at dawn and transferred to a limousine for the ride through the desert.

Even though it had been five years, Farrah recognized the road immediately. 'We're going to Nazaar?' Nazaar, once an important trading post on the frankincense route.

Nazaar, the place where she'd fallen in love.

Tariq gave a faint smile. 'What better place to renew our relationship?'

She turned to face him, her expression exasperated. It had been a long night. She'd dozed on the plane but she was tired and cranky and he was the last man in the world she wanted to be with. 'I don't *want* to renew our relationship, Tariq. And I don't want to go there!' Nazaar held too many memories. It was the birthplace of all her hopes and dreams for the future.

A future that had disintegrated before her eyes.

She'd been hideously, embarrassingly naïve and open with him and she didn't want to be reminded of the fact.

'Nazaar is beautiful. You always said that you loved it.' Unperturbed by her outburst, there was a strange gleam in his eyes that she struggled to interpret.

'I did love it, but that doesn't mean I want to go there now. I want to go home.' She thought of her job at the stables—*the job few people even knew she had*—and felt a pang of anxiety.

She just hated the thought of letting them down. 'I have things that I need to do at home. Commitments.'

'More charity balls that require you to parade half-naked?' His gaze was sardonic. 'If you're worried about missing out on opportunities to dress up, then don't be. You can dress or undress for me as often as you please. I can assure you that I'll be a willing audience. And I know you'll be delighted to know that I've had an entire wardrobe flown over for your entertainment.'

Entertainment? She gaped at him and then reminded herself that the women that he usually mixed with would no doubt have embraced him at this point.

Women like her mother.

It was so unbelievably shallow that she wanted to roll her eyes. 'That sort of gesture may have been enough to guarantee you success with every other woman on the planet,' she said sweetly, 'but it doesn't work with me.'

'I don't think this is the time to explore each other's pasts,' he delivered smoothly and she flopped back against the seat, wondering what it took to deflate his ego.

'Well, that's a good thing,' she snapped, 'because I don't have a past. The good thing about having a brush with a guy like you early in life is that it tends to teach a girl a lesson that she never forgets.'

'If you're suggesting that you've lived the life of a nun since our last meeting then you're wasting your breath,' he drawled lazily. 'No one who saw you parading down the catwalk in that swimming costume would ever accuse you of sexual innocence, *laeela*.'

Realising that she was fast becoming a victim of her own deception, she frowned. 'Tariq—'

'Drop the conversation,' he ordered, a hint of menace in his dark gaze. 'I may be modern enough to accept that you have a past, but it doesn't mean I'm ready to talk about it.'

'There's nothing modern about you, Tariq,' she said flatly,

'You're well and truly stuck in the Stone Age. When it comes to women, the average camel is more advanced than you.'

'I see you still haven't succeeded in curbing your seemingly unquenchable need to verbalize every thought that enters your head,' he observed pleasantly and she gritted her teeth.

'Where I come from, women are allowed to speak.'

'They're allowed to speak where I come from too,' Tariq responded instantly, 'only those with sense learn to measure the impact of their words before they utter them. You might want to give it a try some time.'

'If you don't like the way I am then there's a simple solution,' she said flippantly. 'Turn round and drop me back at the airport.'

'I like the way you are.' There was amusement in his gaze and his tone was deceptively mild. 'If I didn't, then I wouldn't be marrying you.'

'You're *not* marrying me!' She turned to him, frustrated and goaded by his inability to listen to her. 'I don't know why you've suddenly decided that I'm "the one", but it isn't going to work, I can tell you that now. So you might as well turn this car around before I disrupt your life again.'

'Let's stop fighting.' Tariq slid an arm across the back of the seat, his long, strong fingers hovering within touching distance of her neck. 'I agree that we need time together before we get married. That is why we are going to Nazaar and not to my palace at Fallouk. It will give us time to get to know each other again without others interfering.'

'Again? You never knew me, Tariq. And I don't need a break with you! I don't want a break! I have things to do. I have to go to wo—' She broke off quickly, realizing just how much of herself she'd been about to reveal. She'd almost confessed that she had a job! But that was something she would *never* share with him. She was never revealing a single part of herself again! Why would she, when this man had hurt her *so* badly? She didn't care that he thought she was nothing more than a frivolous, empty-headed socialite. His opinion of her didn't matter. All that mattered was keeping herself safe from hurt.

'There are places that I need to be,' she muttered. 'I have a life back in England.'

He looked at her, a hint of amusement in his dark gaze. 'A life that will be outmatched by what I am offering? As my wife, you will have ample opportunity to indulge your passion for retail therapy and numerous social occasions that demand that you dress up and play princesses.'

'And that's all you want in a wife?' He obviously hadn't changed one bit, she thought, struggling to keep the contempt out of her expression. He still expected a woman to be decorative and nothing more.

Something flickered in his eyes but he turned his head away and gave a careless shrug of his broad shoulders. 'I need a queen and part of the role is entertaining. It's important to select someone who is up to the job.'

The *job*? She had to stop her jaw from dropping. How could he be so unromantic? 'And suddenly you've decided that I qualify?'

Her sarcasm appeared lost on him. 'You have learned how to conduct yourself in public.'

The less than subtle reminder that she'd done and said all the wrong things on the last occasion they'd been together brought colour to her cheeks.

'You were ashamed to display me in public.'

'Not any more. This time you'll be by my side when we return to Fallouk.'

She just heard one word.

Fallouk.

She stiffened and her eyes were suddenly wary. 'I don't want to go to Fallouk,' she said huskily. 'I hate Fallouk.'

'It is our capital city. I hardly need remind you that my main residence is there. Any time we spend at Nazaar can only be temporary.' The chill in his tone and the arrogant tilt of his head reminded her that Tariq bin Omar al-Sharma had been born a prince and would die a prince. Five years before, she'd thought she knew the man. *She'd fallen in love with the man she believed him to be.* But she'd been wrong.

So wrong.

'Your palace is full of politics and intrigue,' she said flatly, 'and frankly I've got better things to do with my time than walk around watching my back all the time.'

His eyes gleamed with amusement. 'I'd forgotten that you have a tendency towards drama. Whenever a group of people gather together you have politics. It is part of the rich tapestry of life. You are being naïve to expect otherwise.'

She didn't need him to remind her of that. 'Well, I've never been that into tapestries. And I found the palace stifling.'

Not to mention bitchy, but she didn't see the point of raising that.

There was a curious expression in his eyes. 'Why are women so contrary? You love to dress up and my palace will afford you ample opportunity and yet you are looking at me as though I just promised to imprison you in a dark dungeon with no food or water.'

She wondered whether it was worth sharing with him that a dark dungeon would be preferable to an hour in the company of his aunts and cousins and decided not.

'Well, maybe you just don't know me as well as you think. You never took the trouble to ask what I cared about, did you, Tariq? You didn't know what I liked and what I didn't like. Let's be honest about this, shall we? All you were ever interested in was sex.'

He studied her carefully, his expression maddeningly impassive. 'You're an extremely beautiful woman,' he drawled softly, 'and the physical attraction between us is powerful, no matter how much you would like to deny its existence. It is clear to me now that you were just too young to handle such an explosive passion. You misunderstood your feelings. It happens.'

He was so cynical about women that he'd failed to spot the real thing, she thought numbly as she looked away, trying to ignore the empty, hollow feeling deep inside her. It wasn't even worth trying to explain that all her life men had been showing interest in her money and, later, her looks. Never, until Tariq, had she met a man who'd seemed interested in her as a person.

But it hadn't been real, of course. He hadn't really been interested in her. The art of conversation and appearing interested were all part of his superior seduction technique. After all, she mused, was there anything more seductive than someone who appeared to find you fascinating? Who appeared to share your interests? Probably not, and she'd fallen for it. The brief memory of how stupid she'd been was enough to harden her resolve.

She'd been stupid once. It didn't mean she had to give a repeat performance.

'It doesn't matter what I think of your palace, because I'm not going there.' She said the words aloud as much for herself as for him and there was steel and determination in her voice as she turned to look at him. 'I want you to order them to turn this car round and I want you to take me back to the airport right now.'

His gaze was tolerant, as if he found her mildly entertaining. 'Naturally, you are surprised by my proposal. You need time to become accustomed to the idea and I intend to give you that time. There will be no wedding until you are sure.'

His belief in himself was monumental. Briefly, she wondered what it would be like to have such unshakeable self-confidence.

'There will be no wedding at all! And taking me to Nazaar isn't going to make any difference to the way I feel about that.' She gritted her teeth and her eyes flashed. 'We could spend a century together, Tariq, and still I wouldn't want to marry you.'

'And yet once,' he reminded her in a soft, lethal tone, 'you dreamed of nothing else.'

The fact that he was aware of her most intimate secrets was deeply humiliating.

'That was before I knew what a total bastard you are.'

The sudden touches of colour that appeared high on his aristocratic cheek bones offered the only indication of his disapproval. 'As I have already said to you, Farrah, be careful. My patience is not limitless and you've clearly failed to learn the art of diplomacy over the years. Your desire to shock and flirt with danger does you no credit.'

'Which just goes to prove that I would be deeply unsuitable as a wife,' she said helpfully, 'so you might as well just turn this car round now. Either that or just instruct your bodyguards to shoot me and have done with it.'

'On the contrary, I have decided that you have all the qualities that I require in a wife.'

Her heart was thumping. 'You want a shocking wife?'

'A certain independence of spirit is to be admired.' His slow smile was unmistakably masculine. 'And fire and passion is always a bonus in the bedroom—'

'Which is the only place a woman has a role, in your opinion.' She felt her face flame and dragged her eyes away from his. 'Be careful you don't take on more than you can handle, Tariq.'

'I have never in my life had trouble handling a woman.'

'And you've certainly had enough practice,' she muttered, unable to hide the hurt and the pain.

He'd dated some of the most beautiful women in the world. Why she'd once thought she meant something to him was beyond her. She must have been really, *really* foolish at the age of eighteen.

Thank goodness she'd grown up and seen the light.

'You have no reason to feel jealous. You are the one I'm marrying.'

'I'm not jealous, Tariq. To be jealous you have to care and I don't care about you. You have no effect on me whatsoever.'

His movement was swift and smooth and came without warning. In a show of ruthless determination and masculine strength, he powered her back against the seat and trapped her mouth under his with such ferocious passion that her whimper of shock was swiftly transformed into a soft sigh of acquiescence.

Her skin tingled, heat exploded deep within her and every inch of her trembling, quivering body cried out for him. *Ached for him*.

It had been five years since they'd touched and yet it was as if her senses had retained a memory of him.

She'd dreamed so often of the two of them together. Had tried to imagine what it would be like to be with him properly. And they'd come close. *So close—*

Until he'd stopped it.

But he wasn't stopping it now and his hard body came down on hers, one muscular thigh sliding between her legs as he held her captive with his weight and the heat of his mouth. The hard thrust of his arousal touched her intimately and she shifted and arched in an attempt to bring them closer together.

She felt hot. *So hot*. Her body burned and craved. Her heart bumped against her chest and the blood raced around her body. Her fevered senses demanded that she do something to relieve the pounding, pulsing tension that throbbed deep in her pelvis.

Frustration and anticipation exploded inside her and she moved against him in an instinctive invitation that was entirely feminine.

She needed him and that need was a powerful driving force that blasted everything from her head except the primal urge for sexual fulfilment.

Dragging her mouth from his, she breathed his name and then slid her arms round his neck, traced the roughness of his jaw with the tip of her tongue and then found his mouth again.

Accepting her fevered overtures, his tongue delved between her parted lips and he muttered something that she didn't understand, sliding his hand beneath her hips to haul her closer still to his powerful frame.

With a gasp of encouragement she wrapped her legs around him and then sobbed with frustration as she realized that the thin silk of her trousers still separated them.

She reached out to touch him, her hands fumbling in her haste, but he lifted his mouth from hers and eased himself away from her seeking fingers. His eyes glittered dark and dangerous as he gazed down at her, a frown on his impossibly handsome face.

'This is *not* the right time—'

'Tariq—'

'When the time is right, you will give yourself to me and it will be good. But this is not that time.' His voice slightly husky, he sat up in a smooth movement and relaxed against the seat. Nothing about his body language suggested that only moments before they'd been on the verge of indulging in hot, mindless sex on the back seat of his car.

Torn between aching frustration and utter humiliation that he still had the control to pull away, she smoothed the jacket of her suit and waited for the hot colour in her cheeks to subside before turning to look at him.

The exotic, angular planes of his handsome face revealed nothing. As usual, his expression gave no clues as to what he was thinking. If their torrid encounter had affected him at all then there was no evidence of that fact.

By contrast, her lips felt swollen and hot and her whole body was still suffering the shocking after-effects of their erotic interlude.

'Why did you do that?' Her voice was hoarse and she just hated herself for revealing so much despite her best intentions. *'Why?'*

He turned to her, his gaze faintly mocking. 'Because you insist on pretending that there is nothing between us when we both know that we share a powerful bond. You are a complex woman. On the one hand you are almost painfully honest and yet when it comes to our relationship you are happy to deceive yourself. I wanted to prove something and I did.'

'That's rubbish.' Ignoring the insistent throb that tortured the very centre of her body, she slid into the corner of her seat, placing herself as far away from him as possible. 'All you've proved is that you're a good kisser. And you jolly well should be. You've certainly had enough practice.'

'I've just proved that, when I decide the time is right, you will come to my bed willingly.'

'The only way you'll get me anywhere near your bed is if you drag me,' she threw back at him and he smiled.

'I think we both know that isn't going to be necessary.' He was so blisteringly confident of his own attractions that she was suddenly filled with an almost overwhelming desire to slap him again.

Normally she considered herself to be a very easygoing person, but around Tariq she turned into a boiling cauldron of exaggerated emotion.

'Has anyone ever told you that you have a whopping ego?'

'I have a healthy appreciation for my own abilities and achievements. That's a good thing, *laeela*. Unlike the English, I do not consider success to be distasteful.'

And he'd had enormous success, she knew that.

Educated at Eton, Cambridge and Harvard, he'd taken over the running of the country after his father, the Sultan, had suffered a stroke. And all were in agreement that, thanks to his exceptional business talents, the oil rich state of Tazkash had moved into a new age of peace and prosperity.

She licked her lips. 'So why do you suddenly feel the need to get married?'

He turned to look at her, his dark eyes slumbrous. 'Because it is time. I am ready to take a wife.'

Take a wife. She ignored the sudden warmth that oozed

through her traitorous body. 'Your views on marriage are positively Neolithic. You don't get married just because the alarm clock is buzzing,' she said, her tone thick with contempt, 'you get married for love. But that's something you don't know anything about, do you, Tariq? So tell me, why me? I'm not so stupid as to believe that you care about me, so why have you picked me for the dubious honour of matrimony?'

'It's not true to say that I don't care about you. The connection between us is very strong. We will be good together. I can feel it and so can you.'

Her flesh still yearned for his touch and she shifted in her seat, denying the insistent throb deep in her pelvis. 'No, we wouldn't be good. We'd be a total nightmare.'

He gave a faint smile. 'Are you still so naïve that you don't recognize powerful chemistry between a man and a woman?'

Something dark and dangerous shimmered inside her. Temptation. Shocking, delicious temptation. *Oh, yes, she recognized the chemistry.* And that was the reason that she knew she had to get away from him. 'I could never be happy with you, Tariq.'

'I think I just proved you wrong.'

'You're talking about sex again but marriage is supposed to be about so much more than sex. It isn't going to happen. For the first time in your life you're going to have to come to terms with hearing the word *no*.' And that was going to take some practice, she thought dryly. He was the Sultan. No one dared to say no to him. Everyone around him bowed and scraped and rushed to do his bidding.

He saw, he coveted, he took.

She lay back against the seat, still dazed and disorientated from his kiss and feeling exhausted after such lengthy exposure to his autocratic, forceful personality. Being with Tariq could never be described as restful, she thought desperately, as she tried to subdue the feelings that were still tumbling through her sensitized body.

Nothing had changed. He still only had to touch her for her to lose all sense of reason.

Being around him was dangerous. She didn't trust herself, *didn't trust her body*, not to respond.

But this time she knew that it was just physical, she reminded herself, staring out of the window to hide her confusion. And once she'd got away from him, the squirming, nagging ache deep in her belly would fade to nothing but a distant memory. She'd be able to forget him.

And she had every intention of getting away.

If he wouldn't take her back to the airport, then she'd have to find another way to get herself home.

And the airport wouldn't be an option. Even if she did make her own way there, she'd be stopped the moment she showed her face.

No. She had to find her way into the neighbouring state of Kazban. Nazaar was less than a four hour drive from the border. If she could cross safely into Kazban then she stood a chance of getting home. She was an intelligent, independent woman. How hard could it be?

Preoccupied with planning, she was silent for a while, but not once was she able to forget his presence beside her.

She watched the dunes roll out into the distance, a strangely beautiful alien land that had captured her heart and her imagination from the first moment. She watched as the sun rose higher in the sky and played with the colour of the sand. Burnt orange, browns and yellows all merged together as the wind breathed life into the dunes, creating strange ridges and patterns.

The desert had always fascinated her and it fascinated her still.

'There is a storm coming.' He spoke the words quietly. 'It is predicted to hit in the next twenty-four hours.'

A storm?

She'd never witnessed a sandstorm but she knew that they

could be lethal, obscuring roads and reducing visibility to zero. *And turning the desert into a deathtrap*.

It would affect her plans. She couldn't travel in a storm, she thought, and then her mind moved one step further. On the other hand, who would follow her or even notice her absence if the weather conditions were severe?

With the right sort of four-wheel drive vehicle and satellite navigation, it could be done.

'Have you ever been in the desert in a storm?' She turned to him and his eyes narrowed.

'Of course. I have lived in this country for most of my life and I know the desert as well as I know the city. Far from being romantic, I can assure you that it is an experience to be avoided. Fortunately we have sophisticated weather equipment that allows us to predict such an event with a fair degree of accuracy and behave accordingly. No one would choose to be out in the desert in a storm.'

No one, Farrah thought silently, except a woman who was desperate.

And she was truly desperate.

She sat back in her seat, decision made.

She was going to take a four-wheel drive, cross the border and return home.

And His Royal Highness, Sultan Tariq bin Omar al-Sharma was going to have to look elsewhere for a bride.

Women.

Why did they always have to play such elaborate games?

Why did they have to be so difficult, their actions so utterly incomprehensible?

Having spent the entire journey to Nazaar engaged in verbal warfare, Tariq paced the tent in barely contained exasperation, his dark hair still damp from the shower, the fine silk of his shirt clinging to the muscles of his broad shoulders.

It was so obvious that she was as hot for him as he was for her and yet she persisted in her ridiculous pretence that she had no desire to marry him.

Of *course* she wanted to marry him.

Why wouldn't she?

Marriage was what she'd *always* wanted. What every woman ultimately wanted.

The past still lay between them, he decided with a frown. Once, five years previously, he'd refused to offer her marriage and obviously he'd dented her pride. She was playing games.

But, unfortunately for her, he knew everything there was to know about women's games. He'd had firsthand experience of them since he'd been old enough to speak. And Farrah was no different from all the other women he'd ever known.

Of course, in an ideal world he wouldn't have chosen to *marry* her but, given what he stood to gain from such a union, he was more than prepared to make the sacrifice, particularly now he'd been reacquainted with her charms.

Remembering her uninhibited reaction in the back of the car, he gave a smile. He knew *exactly* which buttons to press and now he had her here at Nazaar, he had all the opportunity he needed to press them as often as necessary.

CHAPTER FIVE

ANGRY with Tariq and exhausted from the drive, Farrah followed six female servants into the tent that had been allocated for her use.

As she was led through folds of creamy canvas, across richly carpeted floor, her anger fell away.

The room was enchanting. Dreamy. And richly exotic. Much more so than the one she'd occupied during her stay five years previously.

The huge bed was draped in silks and velvets and piled high with sumptuous cushions that just invited a person to collapse into their welcoming comfort, a canopy of filmy fabric providing just a suggestion of privacy for the occupant.

No roughing it for Tariq, she thought dryly as she looked at the carefully selected books on the low table next to the bed, the handcrafted furniture and the mixture of traditional ornaments.

Outside the wind was rising and she could hear the faint scrape of sand against the canvas of the tent.

A storm was coming.

And that storm would hide her escape.

Eager to rest while she could, she dismissed the hovering staff, lay down on the bed and slept.

When she woke she was feeling much refreshed.

'His Royal Highness sends his apologies.' A pretty girl

entered the tent and gave her a shy smile. 'He has pressing business matters to attend to and is unable to join you for lunch. But he wants you to know that he will take dinner with you later.'

Oh, no, he wouldn't, Farrah thought to herself, because she wasn't going to be here for dinner. By dinner time she'd be at the airport in neighbouring Kazban, negotiating to be allowed on the first flight back to London.

She wasn't hungry, but she knew it was important that she eat something. She was going to need energy and she needed to take some food with her. It came as a relief to discover that Tariq wouldn't be joining her.

'It doesn't matter. I'm quite happy to have lunch here. I'm thirsty, could I possibly have more water, please?' Water, she knew, would be a key part of her escape. No one in their right mind would risk a journey across the desert without water.

She dined alone and managed to stash away the food and water that she needed. Then it was just a question of waiting until the maids left her alone in the tent.

Although the wind had risen, there was no sign of the promised storm as she made her way through the bright sunshine to where the vehicles were parked.

In terror of being caught at any moment, her heart banging painfully against her ribs, she sidled up to the nearest one and saw the keys in the ignition. With a sigh of relief, she opened the door gingerly and slid inside.

There was no sign of anyone. No guards. No one, but still she winced as the engine burst into life with a throaty roar.

Expecting to be stopped at any moment, she put her foot hard on the accelerator and aimed for the road.

A labyrinth of sand dunes stretched ahead of her but she kept her eyes fixed on the dusty track that she knew led towards the border and the neighbouring state of Kazban. And safety.

Just drive, Farrah, she told herself grimly. Drive and don't look back.

* * *

'Miss Tyndall has gone, Your Highness.'

'Gone?'

Hasim clasped his hands in front of him, his expression that of a man who would have preferred to be elsewhere. 'It appears she has taken one of the four-wheel drive vehicles and has driven into the desert. Alone. It seems entirely possible that she wasn't as excited at the prospect of marriage as you originally predicted.'

Lost for words for possibly the first time in his adult life, Tariq found himself in the grip of an entirely new emotion. Shock. And surprise. Never before had a woman chosen to walk away from him. He had always been the one to do the walking away. He had been the one to end each relationship when he decided that the time was right.

It hadn't occurred to him that she would go to such lengths to avoid him and he frowned in incredulous disbelief, forced to concede that he had clearly misjudged the situation badly.

But why would she reject him when her response to him was so powerful?

With single-minded focus, he traced back through their conversations and his mind came to an emergency stop at one word. Love. Somewhere in their conversation hadn't she flung in the fact that he didn't love her? Was that what was holding her back from saying yes?

With startling clarity, everything suddenly became clear and he cursed himself for his own stupidity and lack of vision.

At the age of eighteen Farrah Tyndall had been a dreamy-eyed romantic and clearly nothing had changed.

She'd loved the legend of Nadia and her Sultan. She'd sighed and smiled over the wonder of their relationship and had been appalled at the Sultan for refusing to marry his love.

For her it had been all about love and romance and not about practicalities.

Cursing himself for crass stupidity, Tariq winced as he

recalled just how lacking in emotional embellishment his proposal of marriage had been. He knew only too well that some women had a deep-seated need to engulf every relationship in a bubble of emotion and he also knew that Farrah was one of those women. He should have remembered that at the age of eighteen all she had done was talk about love.

How could he have made such a mistake? This was a business deal, after all, and he excelled at negotiating business deals. He was a master at evaluating his opponent and pressing all the right buttons. Only in this case he'd totally missed the mark.

It was immediately clear to him that he hadn't made his proposal of marriage anywhere near romantic enough to appeal to the dreamy nature of a girl like Farrah.

But the situation was retrievable, he assured himself, providing he found her before she drove the four-wheel drive into a sand hole or turned it over.

The thought sent a chill down his spine.

Suddenly the need to reach her before something happened to her seemed increasingly urgent.

His expression grim, he turned to his adviser. 'What is the weather forecast?'

'Not good, Your Highness. The wind is rising.'

'All the same, even in good conditions she knows *nothing* about driving in sand.'

'I shall arrange a search party,' Hasim murmured but Tariq shook his head.

'No. I will go myself.'

And hopefully she would see it as a romantic gesture on his part, he thought dryly.

Hasim didn't hide his shock. 'That would not be a good idea—'

'My plans for Farrah Tyndall did not include her dying in the desert,' Tariq reminded him, his mouth set in a hard line. 'I will take the helicopter.'

Hasim licked dry lips. 'I understand that you have a love of extreme sports, Your Excellency, but it is unsafe to fly and—'

'Life cannot always be safe. She has a head start. There is no other way of reaching her. Was the tracking device on her vehicle switched on?'

Hasim nodded, visibly disturbed by the prospect of Tariq taking the helicopter. 'Yes, Your Excellency. But if you insist on flying, at least allow your staff to accompany you—'

'I will not risk any other lives. With luck I will reach her before she does herself permanent damage. If not—' If not then he'd have ample time in which to regret underestimating the Tyndall heiress.

It took less than an hour for Farrah to admit that driving into the desert alone had been a stupid idea. The 'road' soon vanished under the drifting sand and she was forced to rely on the unfamiliar equipment within the vehicle she'd taken.

She'd let the air out of the tyres as she'd seen others do, but the sand was soft and she gripped the wheel hard as she tried to hold her course up a steep dune. Maybe if she made it to the top, she'd be able to get her bearings. Perhaps the road would be visible.

She hit the accelerator and aimed straight for the top of the dune but, as she felt the vehicle slow and the wheels bed down into the soft sand, she automatically flung the wheel to the right, trying to turn. The world tilted and the wheels bedded in deeper.

She was stuck.

Helpless and frustrated, she sat back in her seat. Stay calm, she told herself firmly. Stay calm. But it was hard to stay calm when the wind was rising, night was falling and there was no prospect of digging herself out.

Intending to see whether she could put something under the

wheels, she slid gingerly out of the vehicle, still concerned about tipping it over.

And then she saw the helicopter. Like a threatening black insect, it raced above the dunes towards her and then set down on a dusty flat patch of desert, the whip of the deadly blades clouding the air with particles of sand. The pilot leaped down and his broad shoulders and muscular physique left her in no doubt as to his identity.

Tariq.

She swallowed hard and felt her heart bang against her chest. Which was worse? she wondered helplessly. Getting lost in the desert, never to be seen again, or being taken back to Nazaar by the man from whom she'd been trying to escape?

She braced herself as he reached her and lifted her chin. 'I'm not coming back with you.'

His robes billowed out behind him in the strong wind and his handsome face was hard and devoid of humour. 'I accept that I have made many mistakes in my dealings with you but this is not the time for such a discussion. Had you forgotten that a storm was forecast?'

'No.' The wind whipped her blond hair across her face and she reached up and anchored it with her hand, her eyes narrowed against the wind and the sand. 'I hadn't forgotten. But I thought you wouldn't follow me in a storm.'

He looked momentarily stunned at her confession. 'My proposal of marriage is that abhorrent to you?'

'Where I come from, marriage should be about love, Tariq, and we don't love each other. I don't want you in my life. I tried that once before and it didn't work out.' Even as she spoke, the wind rose and swept harsh, biting sand into their faces. She choked and tried to cover her face with her arms and he muttered something that she didn't understand.

The next thing she knew he was wrapping a soft strip of silk around her mouth and nose with firm but gentle hands.

'This will help. We need to get out of here while we still can. There will be time for talk later.'

'I'm *not* going with you, Tariq.'

He braced himself against the wind and stared at her with naked incredulity, clearly at a loss. 'You would rather stay here and risk death?'

'Than be bullied by you? Yes.'

He stared at her with ill-concealed exasperation. 'I give you my word that, once we have spoken, if you wish to return to London then I will fly you there myself. Is that good enough?'

'What if you're lying?'

Those dark eyes flashed a warning. 'You question my word?'

The wind howled in her ears and, despite the scarf, the sand stung her eyes and seemed to find its way through her clothing to her sensitive skin. Suddenly she realized just how bleak and dangerous their surroundings were. 'All right. Let's get out of here. Back to the helicopter.'

'No helicopter. The conditions are now too dangerous. Visibility is reducing by the minute and I cannot lift off in this.'

'Then what do you propose?'

'We use your four-wheel drive.'

She glanced at it guiltily. 'Ah, well, there's just a bit of a problem with that. I was just getting out to see if I could do something about it.'

He looked at her feet for the first time and his mouth tightened into a grim line. 'In sandals? Don't you know the risks of walking in the desert like that? This isn't London, *laeela*,' he said with sardonic bite. 'Here you walk amongst snakes and scorpions.'

Snakes and scorpions? She squashed down a ridiculously girly instinct to leap up on him and cling round his neck so that her feet were well out of harm's way. The truth was she hadn't been thinking about the desert dangers when she'd planned her escape. She'd been thinking only of him. And getting away.

'The car is stuck,' she muttered and he breathed out sharply.

'The car,' he informed her helpfully, 'is not designed to go sideways down a dune.'

'Well, I know that! I didn't go sideways on purpose! I was aiming for the top but the wheels were just digging deeper and deeper—'

'If you failed to go forwards then you should have gone backwards. Driving in shifting sand, particularly sand that has been softened by the heat of the sun, presents particular challenges. I will move the vehicle and we will return to the camp in that.'

Searching for the rest of his entourage, she glanced over his shoulder and saw no one. 'Where are your bodyguards?'

'There is a storm coming and this is the last place anyone should be because there is no shelter.'

'But you flew—'

'You are my responsibility. I cannot allow others to risk their lives to save yours. The visibility was good when I left Nazaar. But we won't be able to take off again. We will need to return in the four-wheel drive.'

It was her turn to be surprised. He'd come for her alone? 'Your fancy car is totally stuck.'

'Then we will need to unstick it.'

From the gleam in his dark eyes she had a feeling that he was relishing the challenge. Instead of appearing disturbed by the rising wind and the sharp sting of sand against their faces, he merely wrapped something over his own mouth and set to work. Then he slid into the driver's seat and proceeded to manoeuvred the vehicle out of the sand.

He let still more air out of the tyres and then did something clever with the brake, the accelerator and the steering wheel and the vehicle finally sprang to life. Watching the smooth, confident movement of his strong hands, she realized that he made it look easy. And he'd made it look easy five years earlier. Which was why she'd thought that she'd be able to do it herself.

'I was silly to try and drive on my own,' she conceded, clutching the seat as he roared to the top of the dune. 'But you made it look easy.'

'I was born here.' His hands were hard on the wheel and she gave a soft gasp of alarm as they crested the dune. The sand fell away steeply and she clutched at her seat, her eyes wide.

'Tariq—you can't go down there; it's a cliff!'

'Are you afraid?' He turned to her with a gleam of challenge in his eyes. 'I've never asked you if you like roller coasters, *laeela*,' he purred. 'But I'm about to find out. Hold on to your seat.'

Grateful that the swirl of sand obscured at least part of the vertiginous drop, Farrah gripped the seat tightly. 'I hope you're at least half as skilled as you are confident,' she muttered. 'Otherwise we're going to be ending our days at the bottom of this dune.'

Concentrating on the driving, he didn't look towards her but there was a smile on his mouth as he manipulated the wheel with a sure and skilful touch and she realized with a flash of shock that he was enjoying himself. 'There are many things you don't know about me, Farrah, but we are going to remedy that.'

Somehow they were safely down and only then, as the nose of the vehicle rose and she felt the tyres bite into a more solid surface, did she realize that she'd been holding her breath.

'I'm almost relieved I didn't make it to the top,' she muttered. 'If I had, I wouldn't have known what to do about coming down.'

'You should never turn. Turning too sharply has the same effect as slamming on the brakes. If you drive even at a slight angle, the weight transfer is to the downhill wheels which dig in and make the angle even worse. You will roll over. I know.' He dealt her a wicked smile. 'I did it several times when I was younger.'

The smile made her heart and stomach flip in unison and she issued herself a sharp reminder about the dangers of falling for the charms of the Desert Prince.

He'd always enjoyed risking life and limb—she remembered that now. Remembered reading that he'd been forced to curb his more dangerous activities once he'd become the ruler of Tazkash.

'I've driven a four-wheel drive before and I thought it would be similar.'

'Driving on a sliding, shifting surface takes much skill.' He glanced across at her. 'Drive too fast and you'll rush into quicksand or a sinkhole, drive too slowly and you won't have the momentum to get up the slope.'

Hearing him spell out the difficulties, she realized how foolish she'd been even to think about driving into the desert. Gloomily, she stared out of the window, frowning as she saw the sky darken and the visibility reduce. 'The storm is getting worse.'

'And we are less than twenty minutes from Nazaar and safety. You can relax, *laeela*.'

'Twenty minutes? That's not possible.' She glanced at him, shocked. 'I'd been driving for over two hours.'

'In circles. You were lost.' His eyes were fixed on the road and she studied his strong, handsome profile, wondering if he'd ever had a crisis of confidence in his life.

'How can you possibly know that when you weren't there?'

'Because the vehicle is equipped with a tracking device. That was how I was able to find you so easily.'

Realising that she'd never stood a chance, she flopped back against her seat. 'Why me, Tariq?' Impulsively she turned to him. 'I can't understand why you would suddenly want to marry me. You, who always hated the idea of marrying anyone. Why me and why now?'

'Because it is right.' He brought the vehicle to a halt in a cloud of dusty sand and immediately a horde of people descended on them. Briefly his eyes met hers. 'This is not a conversation for now. You will dine with me tonight and we will talk.'

* * *

Mildly embarrassed at everyone's relief at their safe return, Farrah accepted the offer of a scented bath and a massage and then slipped back to the sanctuary of her luxurious canopied room. Her scalp still tingled from the application of shampoos and scented oils and her hair fell damp and glossy over her shoulders.

A girl, who introduced herself as Yasmina, had been sent to help her dress and for once Farrah didn't resist. She felt completely exhausted, but whether from the strain of her ride through the desert or the stress of being back with Tariq again, she wasn't sure.

All she knew was that she didn't have the energy to resist when the girl started to dry and brush her hair.

'You have beautiful hair. It is easy to understand why His Highness requested that it be left loose this evening,' the girl murmured as her hands stroked and soothed.

In receipt of that totally inflammatory piece of information, Farrah tried to summon up the energy to instruct the girl to fasten her hair up on her head, but she decided that she'd had enough confrontation for one day.

Instead, she reminded herself that Tariq had promised to fly her back to London if that was what she wanted. And that *was* what she wanted, she told herself firmly. So she'd dine with him and make sure that he got that message, get some rest and then travel home in the morning.

Satisfied with the plan, she realized that Yasmina was showing her a dress. 'It is an extremely generous gift from His Highness,' the girl breathed. '*How* he honours you.'

How he fails to understand me, Farrah thought wearily as she allowed the girl to slip the dress over her head. Made of the finest silk, different shades of green and blue merged and blended together like the colours of a peacock feather. The fabric was of such superior quality that it was like wearing nothing next to her skin and Farrah reached down to touch it.

Should she refuse to wear it? Probably, but she had to wear

something and obviously she hadn't been given the opportunity to pack anything of her own.

Yasmina stared at her in admiration. 'You look beautiful enough to ensnare a sultan.'

Farrah frowned as she slipped her feet into strappy sandals. She didn't want to ensnare anyone. She just wanted to go home. Back to her life. *Back to the riding stables*.

And if Tariq thought that one pretty dress was going to change her mind, then he was as far off the mark as he ever had been.

Tariq paced the length of the tent, ignoring the staff who were carefully arranging various delicacies on the low table.

Everything was in place, he thought.

She wanted romance and now, thanks to a sudden flash of inspiration on his part, he had an entire team of staff working flat out to deliver nothing but romantic gestures. Massage, candles, dresses, jewellery—as far as he could see, he was ticking all the boxes. How could he possibly fail?

There were certain courtship rituals that a woman expected and he'd neglected those rituals because he'd thought the connection between them was enough. Clearly it wasn't and he wouldn't be making that mistake again.

When a whisper of silk announced her entrance into his tent he turned to her with a confident smile. The smile froze on his lips as he saw her. Something dangerous and unfamiliar shifted inside him and for a brief moment he forgot that the relationship he was trying to forge with this woman was all about business.

She looked like a woman designed specifically to tempt a man from the straight and narrow. A woman who would wrap herself around a man's mind until all coherent thought had been squeezed out.

The sleek fall of her hair shone pale gold, gleaming under

the flickering light of the candles that had been arranged around the tent by his staff in accordance with his instruction.

Exquisite, he thought to himself, indulging in a brief erotic fantasy that involved all that glorious hair trailing over his heated, naked flesh.

Lust stabbed through him and, with a flash of masculine frustration, he momentarily reflected on the fact that a woman's requirement for romance invariably acted as the brakes on the roller coaster ride towards sexual satisfaction. Before he could take her to bed and give them both what they needed, he was expected to jump through all the right hoops.

But he was well on his way, he assured himself as he dragged his gaze away from her lush, glossy mouth and forced himself to concentrate.

He'd arranged for her to be pampered, he'd presented her with a dress. Now on to the next thing on his list. Compliments and jewellery. Both were easy.

'You look very beautiful.' His voice was soft and he reached for a velvet box in midnight blue that had been delivered only moments earlier. 'I have something for you which I think you'll like.'

She opened the box and he silently congratulated his staff on their excellent taste. The diamond necklace was a truly exquisite piece. Rare and tasteful. Preparing himself to be on the receiving end of an appropriate amount of female gratitude, he dismissed the staff with a wave of his hand and was taken aback when she snapped the box shut and slipped it into her bag.

'Thank you.'

This was not the reaction he'd expected. 'You're not going to wear it?'

'Possibly. I suppose it depends on the occasion. It seems a bit over the top for dinner in the desert in a tent. To be honest, it's not really my style.'

Never before having witnessed such a lack of enthusiasm for

jewellery, Tariq looked at her with frank incomprehension. 'Diamonds are every woman's style.'

'But I'm not every woman.' She gave him a sympathetic smile and walked gracefully over to the cushions. 'Sorry to be difficult. I'm sure most of your conquests would be well and truly sewn up by now. Pretty dress, candles, diamonds—you should be on to a sure thing.'

Her tone told him that he was missing something crucial and he racked his brains for inspiration. 'They are the things that matter to women.'

'No.' Her smile faded and she looked him straight in the eye. 'They're the things that matter to the women you usually mix with, Tariq. That's not the same thing. I'm not like them and yet you persist in thinking that I am. That's always been your mistake.'

'I don't make mistakes.'

'You're making so many mistakes you're falling over them,' she said sweetly. 'Your mistakes are the reason I drove your car into the desert. We are operating on entirely different wavelengths. It's clear to me now that you will *never* understand me.'

On the receiving end of this less than encouraging announcement, Tariq was filled with a previously unknown urge to defend his actions.

'You are a woman who lives to dress up—'

'So you think.' She sank on to the pile of cushions in a graceful movement and he inhaled deeply, hanging on to his patience with difficulty. Being with a woman was supposed to be relaxing, he mused. But life with Farrah was one long game of cat and mouse. She was infuriatingly unpredictable. Surely he'd done everything that was required of a man? What more did she expect?

'I suppose you have a rich father to buy you all the diamonds you need.'

'Yes.' Reaching forward, she helped herself to a glossy black date. 'But you see, Tariq, I don't need diamonds.' She slid the date into her mouth and he felt tension throb through his body as she licked her fingers. 'Has it ever occurred to you that you and I are actually very similar?'

Disturbed from the pleasurable act of contemplating their differences, Tariq looked at her blankly. 'How?' At that precise moment he wasn't interested in exploring similarities.

'We were both born with sufficient wealth and influence to ensure that we could never be entirely confident of another person's motives.'

Her mouth was perfect, he reflected, struggling to ignore his increasing arousal. 'I don't know what you mean—'

'No. You probably don't.' She reached for another date and popped it into her mouth. 'And that's always been your problem. You don't really care what women think about you because you only connect with them on one level. But I'm not interested in that one level. You have absolutely no idea who I am or what I want and you've never bothered to take the trouble to find out. All you're really interested in is sex.'

And who could blame him?

His eyes still on her mouth, he watched as she sampled the food with slow, sensuous relish. Never before had he watched a woman eat with such obvious enjoyment. All the females he'd ever known had appeared to regard food as a threat and eating as nothing more than a distasteful social obligation to be undertaken under sufferance and preferably without the consumption of a single calorie. Watching Farrah lick her fingers, it was clear that she held an entirely different attitude to food. Showing none of the inhibitions characteristic of her sex, she studied each plate with enthusiasm and helped herself to a selection of local delicacies.

In the grip of a severe attack of lust, Tariq struggled to deliver the conversation that was so clearly required of him. 'Why would you always be suspicious of people's motives?'

'Because I've learned to be that way. And I'm suspicious of

yours, Tariq.' She leaned forward and selected an olive from the bowl in front of her. 'Why would you want to marry me? It doesn't make sense.'

It made perfect sense to him. In fact, as he watched her nibbling and licking her lips, it was making increasing sense. His body was wound so tight that he thought he might explode and it felt as though his entire brain was sliding south. Suddenly there was only one purpose in his life.

He wanted Farrah Tyndall and he wanted her to himself.

And what better way was there of guaranteeing exclusivity than marriage?

Marriage would mean that she could take up permanent residence in his bed. Captive. No other man would have a chance with her. No other man would see her as he was seeing her now, her fair hair trailing on to the cushions, the delicate silk of her dress skimming her amazing body. For the first time in his life he realized that the institution of marriage came with significant benefits.

She would be his. He would own her, body and soul.

At that precise moment he had forgotten that the purpose of his own marriage was supposed to be all about business because all thoughts of business had been blown from his mind. With her lying in front of him he could focus on nothing except pleasure.

'We would be perfect together. You saw that five years ago.' His voice was husky as he lowered himself on to the cushions next to her. 'Am I to be punished because I was a little slower than you to recognize what it was that we had?'

'So you're saying that you've spent the past five years pining for me?' There was a hint of sarcasm in her tone but the tiny pulse beating in her throat told him that she wasn't as cool and indifferent as she pretended to be.

'You weren't the obvious choice of a wife,' he confessed, re-membering that women were purported to like honesty, 'but never has any woman affected me the way you do.' The discovery that the second part of his statement was nothing more than the truth came as something of a shock.

Up until now, the women in his life had been more or less interchangeable. Society clones with the right pedigree. Women paraded in front of him by his family in the hope that he'd select one, marry her and produce the necessary heir.

'Well, if I wasn't the obvious choice five years ago, why would that have changed?'

'Perhaps it is I who have changed,' Tariq muttered, still reeling from the implications of his discovery. It was just because their relationship had never reached the obvious conclusion, he assured himself, a frown touching his black eyebrows. Had the relationship developed in the way he'd anticipated, he would have had no problem moving on in the same way that he'd always moved on. 'I am no longer prepared to marry for political reasons.'

In fact, he wouldn't have been prepared to marry at all were it not for the fact that he was able to seek a divorce after forty days and forty nights.

'You want to take me to bed.'

'If that was all I wanted, then why would I marry you?'

Her gaze was fixed on his. 'I'm still asking myself that question.'

'Then allow me to answer it for you. I have seen enough marriages fail to know that there must be something more than political gain in order to make the relationship work.'

'And yet you never thought that Nadia should have been more than the Sultan's mistress.'

Her voice was pleasant but he tensed, sensing a trap. 'You still think of that legend?' He leaned forward to fill her glass. 'We are not talking about history now. Things change and progress. We are not living the lives of our ancestors.'

'And what would your family think of this marriage you're proposing?' For a brief moment he saw the flash of hurt in her eyes and his eyes narrowed as he remembered the reaction of his family to Farrah Tyndall.

'My family must accept my decision.' And they would, he mused, because the senior members of his family had been informed that the marriage was designed to benefit Tazkash. 'You are my choice. That is all there is to be said.'

'Oh, I'm sure they'll just welcome me with open arms.' She pulled her hand away from his and drew her knees up, her position as defensive as a child. 'Your cousins, uncles, aunts—none of them wanted me near you, Tariq. I was seen as a threat. They made sure that my time in your palace was as unhappy as possible.'

He decided that the pursuit of his goal dictated that he overlook the criticism of his family. 'Because you were the first woman who had ever truly interested me. You threatened them with your outspoken ways and your dazzling looks.'

And by her pedigree.

The reputation of Sylvia Tyndall and her subsequent death had attracted sufficient negative press attention to ensure that her daughter was viewed with the same suspicion.

Farrah lifted her chin. 'Five years ago I would have believed that, but you taught me not to be naïve. You taught me that actions always have a reason. I want to know your reason.'

Why, he asked himself with mounting exasperation, did she pick this particular moment to suddenly discover the meaning of cynicism? 'Once, we were the best of friends. Give me the chance to prove to you that we can be so again. Give me the chance to prove that we'd be good together. Two weeks, that's all I ask. Stay with me for two weeks. If at the end of that time you still wish to return home, then I will arrange it. You have my word.'

'Why would I agree to stay for two weeks?'

He lifted a plate of delicacies that she'd almost finished. 'Because what we have is worth exploring further. No man has made you feel the way I make you feel.'

'You're arrogant.' But he heard the husky edge to her voice and smiled, knowing that he was winning the argument.

'I'm honest, *laeela*. And if I am wrong, how can you lose? In two weeks you can walk away.'

And she'd definitely be walking away in six, leaving him with control of her father's company.

She licked her lips. 'And what are we going to do for two weeks?'

'All the things you enjoyed on your last visit.' Relieved to see her wavering, he kept his tone was warm and persuasive. 'If it helps, think of it as a holiday.'

She hesitated, her eyes on his face. 'I don't think so. A holiday is the last thing I need—'

'Maybe it's exactly what you need. I know that I hurt you. You have never been involved with another man since me,' he said quietly. 'Isn't that true?'

Her eyes widened with shock. 'How do you know that? Are you having me followed?'

He made a mental note to destroy the file he had on her that was currently locked inside his desk back in the palace at Fallouk.

'No, but you still wear my ring.'

Her chin lifted defensively. 'I've already told you why.'

'I don't think so, *laeela*,' Tariq murmured 'You wear the ring because our time together was special. The least you can do is give us a chance to see what might have been.'

She eyed him warily. 'That would make me stupid.'

'That would make you sensible,' he contradicted swiftly, bestowing a smile on her anxious face. She was deliciously transparent and always had been. *She still wanted him but, like a typical woman, she needed to justify the need that burned inside her.* 'If a love is so great that it keeps you from forming a relationship with another man, is it not at least worth another look?'

Their eyes held and he felt the tension rise between them, saw indecision as her mind fought the battle between common sense and the powerful connection between them. The rational and the irrational.

'I can't just take time out of my life without warning,' she muttered finally. I'd have to make some phone calls. I wasn't expecting to take a holiday.'

Wondering how one could take a holiday from a life that contained nothing but social engagements, Tariq gave a nod. 'Of course. You shall make whatever calls are necessary to give you peace of mind.'

Having won the battle, he was willing to make whatever minor concessions were necessary in order to allow her to feel comfortable with her decision.

She must be mad.

Why hadn't she just insisted that he put her on a plane and fly her home? She'd gone into his tent intending to demand exactly that. But somehow he'd talked her into staying.

Appalled at herself, Farrah called the riding school where she worked and explained that she wouldn't be able to come in for two weeks. Then she called a couple of close friends and told them she was going to be travelling for a while.

It wasn't an entirely ridiculous decision, she told herself as she paced the length of her tent, too wound up to even contemplate sleep. Tariq *had* haunted her dreams for five years. He was right when he claimed to be the reason she'd never become involved with another man.

Maybe spending some time with him was just what she needed to help her put him out of her mind, once and for all.

Once she saw that they had nothing in common, it would be easier to walk away.

Having justified what appeared to be an utterly ridiculous decision on her part, she slipped out of her dress and climbed into bed, her mind still spinning. She'd spend the next two weeks doing all the things she enjoyed doing, she decided.

And two weeks of non-stop exposure to Tariq should be more than enough to remind her what a cold-hearted, arrogant individual he was.

And then she'd fly home. And she'd move on.

No more sultans for her.

CHAPTER SIX

THEY spent every day exploring the desert.

Tariq took her dune driving and wadi bashing, speeding along the empty river beds until Farrah gasped at the sheer exhilaration of the experience. And then he let her take a turn behind the wheel and taught her to do it. And he proved to be a gifted and patient teacher as he showed her how to drive in sand, how to alter the tyre pressure and how to use the sophisticated global positioning system.

'If I'd known how to do this a few days ago I'd be back in England now,' she said dryly and he dealt her a smile that was disturbingly attractive.

'Then I'm thankful that I have postponed the lesson until this point. Are you interested in the local wildlife?'

'Snakes and scorpions?'

His smile widened. 'On this occasion, no. I had something more fluffy and appealing in mind.'

'Fluffy and appealing?' Despite her resolutions not to be affected by him, she couldn't stop the laughter. 'Is that another one of your stereotypical views of women? We like the fluffy and appealing?'

'You would, perhaps, prefer the scaly and poisonous?'

She shuddered, still laughing. 'No, thanks. On this occasion I'm happy to fall into the box you've designed.'

'Box?'

'Yes. You put all women in the same little box because you believe that we all have the same characteristics.'

'For you, Farrah,' he said dryly, 'I have designed your own, private box. And now look—' He gestured for her to turn off the engine and leaned across, sliding an arm across her shoulders as he pointed across the sand dunes. 'There. What do you see?'

He was so close she could hardly breathe. Her nose picked up his elusive masculine scent and her eyes were drawn to the dark hair that clustered on his forearms. He had strong arms, she thought absently, trying to concentrate on what he was saying. Following the line of his gaze, she gave a soft gasp of delighted surprise. 'Oh—Tariq.' The animal stood still, eyes huge, as if sensing danger. Even though they were inside the vehicle, Farrah dropped her voice to a whisper. 'It's gorgeous. What is it?'

'A type of gazelle. They were hunted almost to the point of extinction,' he told her, 'but this is now a protected area and the numbers are recovering. That particular project was a success in conservation terms.'

Farrah stared at the creature, fascinated. 'A protected area? It looks like desert—'

'And, of course, it is—' his tone was amused '—but this particular part of the desert is protected. We restrict the amount of off-road driving because it damages the vegetation and threatens the animals. There are several such sites in Tazkash.'

She turned to look at him and caught her breath. His head was close to hers as he leaned forward to get a better look at the animal. The dark stubble on his jaw seemed merely to intensify his masculinity and she swallowed.

'I never knew you were interested in conservation.'

His eyes slid to hers, his gaze faintly mocking. 'As you are always pointing out, there is much that we have yet to discover about each other.' His eyes dropped to her mouth and lingered, leaving her in no doubt that he was referring to more than his dedication to local wildlife. 'It is my responsibility to act as custodian for this country. Part of my job is to protect our heritage for future generations and that includes the wildlife.'

'Your job?'

'Of course.' He gave a casual shrug and withdrew his arm, leaning back against his seat. 'Mine is a job like any other.'

'*Not* like any other,' she said dryly and he smiled.

'Perhaps not. Although, in truth, my role bears similarity to that of any other chief executive of a large organization. It certainly comes with the same number of major headaches.'

And she knew that he'd made an enormous success of the business. 'Most CEOs don't have the autonomy that you have. You just give an order and everyone stumbles over each other to carry it out.'

He threw his head back and laughed in genuine amusement. 'How I wish it were that simple, *laeela*. I spend my life playing politics. Persuading people. Preparing arguments. It's like an ongoing game of chess. I must anticipate every move that my opponent is likely to make and act accordingly. Introducing just small elements of change often requires months, if not years, of careful manoeuvring on my part.'

She looked at him, interested. 'What do you want to change?'

'It is important that Tazkash remains competitive and a real force if our people are to thrive and be safe.' His handsome face was grimly serious. 'But progress must not come at the expense of our heritage. The preservation of our culture is important. My job is to find a way of weaving the past into the future so that the people benefit. Oil will not support us for ever and we need to find alternative ways of generating revenue.'

'You really care about the people who live here.' It was a statement rather than a question and he nodded.

'Of course. It's important to understand the way of life of our people. Where we came from and where we are going. We are used to exploiting a harsh environment and it's important to understand the problems our people face. Lately we have been exploring water courses and irrigation systems—'

She listened in fascination as he outlined the various projects that were currently ongoing to make life easier for the people. And she asked endless questions and added her own thoughts.

Their conversations continued over the days that followed, becoming more complex and stimulating, often lasting well into the night as they ate by the light and warmth of a bonfire.

He taught her to read the stars as his ancestors had once done and showed her how to watch for signs of changes in the weather.

'You love it here, don't you?' She stared at his face, bronzed and handsome in the flickering firelight. Saw him nod.

'In the desert, life is simple.' Idly, he tossed a stick into the fire and watched it flame and crackle. 'I suppose in a different life, this is where I would belong. Where I would choose to be.'

She hid her surprise. She'd assumed that he enjoyed the luxury and pomp that was part of palace life at Fallouk. It hadn't occurred to her that maybe he was playing a part, just as she did.

'I can understand that.' Her voice was soft as she laid back on the cushions and rugs that had been placed by the fire for their comfort. 'It's blissful. I love everything about it.'

'And yet, by now you must be bored. You don't have to pretend with me.' He shot her an amused glance. 'You are young and very beautiful. I'm sure you must be missing your usual round of parties. Here in the desert, we lack that many excuses to dress up.'

Part of her wanted to tell him the truth—confess that she hated the constant round of parties and meaningless mingling. But he was a man who expected a woman to fulfil that role—expected a woman to be like her mother. Having been so utterly consumed by Tariq in the past, *having trusted him enough to bare her very soul to him*, could she risk giving him a glimpse of what lay behind the glittering shell that she'd so carefully created? Did she dare confide her innermost secrets? No. Such a confession would make her too vulnerable. Fortunately she'd grown so used to concealing her true self from all but a few close friends that deception came easily. 'The desert has many charms,' she said finally, 'and life isn't all about parties, although I do miss my friends, of course. I have a few good friends that I've had from childhood and I'd trust them with my life. I've learned to be wary of strangers. Haven't you? Is there anyone that you truly trust, Tariq?' She turned her head towards him. Saw the tension in his broad shoulders.

When he finally answered, his voice was quiet. 'No,' he replied. 'There isn't. But that is the price you pay for being in my position.'

She couldn't imagine being without her friends. 'It's a high price.'

'Not to me. I've never felt the need to confide in people.'

'Everyone needs someone,' Farrah said softly, wriggling into a more comfortable position on the rug. 'Being loved for who you truly are is the best thing in the world. The only thing that really matters. The rest of it—the money, the lifestyle, that isn't real.' She knew that better than anyone. *Had seen her mother seduced and destroyed by the empty glamour.*

'I thought you loved all the glitter and bright lights.'

She quickly realized how much she'd betrayed. 'I do,' she said hastily, 'but there are other things that matter too…' Her voice trailed off and he lifted an eyebrow in question.

'So—' his voice was low and persuasive, his eyes gleaming dark in the firelight '—what else matters to you, Farrah Tyndall?'

For a moment she thought about the children she worked with. About her job at the riding school and the fact that no one knew who she really was. How her identity, her money, didn't matter. But her other life was her last defense. She had to keep that part of herself locked away from him. 'Oh—er—'she struggled to think of something plausible '—charity work, that sort of thing.' She sounded intentionally vague and he studied her for a moment, his dark eyes searching.

'You can do charity work in Tazkash if that is what you wish. As my wife, it would be expected of you.'

Her heart flipped. Every angle of his strong, handsome face was designed to make an artist drool. He was every inch the arrogant prince and she couldn't look at him without catching her breath. Being so close to him for the past two weeks had been a delicious kind of torture. But he hadn't touched her. Not once. This was the first time he'd mentioned marriage since the night of her attempted escape and her reaction worried her. She should have leaped to her feet and run for cover; instead, she felt drawn to him. 'Your wife?' Just saying the words sent a thrill running through her body and she closed her eyes to hide what she was feeling.

She'd done it again.

Despite her best intentions, despite everything that had gone before, she'd let herself fall in love with him again. She'd opened her heart and let him in.

Not the Sultan, she realized as she opened her eyes and looked at him. She'd never been interested in his status. Like Nadia, she'd fallen in love with the man, not the title or the promise of riches. It was the man who interested her. The man that she saw whenever they were here at Nazaar. There was a part of him that he only seemed to reveal in the desert.

He was watching her. 'We agreed not to talk about it for two weeks. That time is up tomorrow. Until then the subject is banned.'

She stared at him, suddenly uncertain. Did he still want her? Was he intending to renew his proposal? Or had two weeks in the desert with her been enough to convince him once more that she was unsuitable wife material? Suddenly she needed to change the subject. 'Did your parents bring you here when you were young?'

He tensed and a muscle flickered in his strong jaw. 'No. My mother loved life in the Palace. She would rather have died than spend time in the desert. She needed civilization at all times.'

It was the first time he'd ever mentioned his mother. The first time he'd ever told her anything remotely personal about himself. Maybe it was the darkness or maybe it was the intimacy of the conversation, but suddenly she felt truly close to him for the first time. It was just the two of them and the crackling fire. 'And your father?'

'My father was busy with affairs of state.'

'But you were his only child. He must have spent some time with you.'

His face was expressionless. 'Raising a child wasn't his role.'

'What about playing with you? Reading to you?' She thought of her own father and the hours of fun they'd had together. 'Surely you must have spent some time together?'

'He allocated time each week to teach me what he thought I'd need to know about ruling Tazkash.'

Ruling? She wanted to ask about play. Wanted to know whether he'd ever had any fun with his parents, but the answer was in his face. 'That sounds pretty lonely.' She felt a twist of sympathy for what he'd missed.

'On the contrary—' he gave a bitter laugh '—to be lonely would have been a blessing. I was surrounded by staff from the moment I was born. I had three nannies, several tutors and a whole team of bodyguards briefed to watch my every move. To be lonely was never more than an elusive dream.'

'You can be surrounded by people and still be lonely,' she said quietly. 'If the people around you don't love and understand you, then you can be extremely lonely.'

'Are you speaking from experience?'

Her eyes flew to his. 'No, I—' She broke off and licked her lips as she tried to make good her mistake. 'My father worked very hard, of course, but my mother was always around.'

'You are close to your father?'

'He's my hero,' she said simply, reaching her hands towards the warmth of the fire. 'Despite her faults he adored my mother, and he never found another woman who meant the same to him. He brought me up to believe in one special love and never to settle for anything less.'

She couldn't read his expression. 'That's a very romantic view.'

'It's how it was for my parents,' Farrah said quietly. 'Tell me how you came to spend time in the desert. If your parents didn't bring you here, then who did?'

His eyes lifted to hers and he stared at her for a long moment. 'When I was seven, one of my tutors decided that I needed to broaden my education, to understand my roots and the ways of our people. He brought me to Nazaar.'

'And you loved it.'

'Oh, yes.' He leaned over and topped up her glass. 'I shall steal one of your over-the-top romantic expressions and say that it was love at first sight.'

She lifted an eyebrow in mockery. 'Getting soppy on me, Tariq?'

'Perhaps.' He flashed her a smile that was so charismatic she felt her stomach perform a series of acrobatic moves. 'Blame the stars.'

She stared up at the tiny dots that sparkled and patterned the sky. 'Did your parents love each other? Were they happy together?'

He hesitated. 'To answer that, I will have to shatter your romantic illusions. They were *extremely* unhappy. And the result of that was that they spent virtually no time together. It was very much a marriage of political convenience.'

'Then it's no wonder you don't believe in love.'

His eyes narrowed. 'How do you know I don't believe in love?'

'Nadia and the Sultan.' She sat up and rested her chin on her knees, her expression dreamy. 'When we talked about it you always disagreed with me. You could never understand the degree of passion that might make death seem a better option than losing the love of your life. You were always practical. Now I understand why.'

'Perhaps I just don't believe that marriage is the only way of expressing true passion.'

'Ah—so finally we're back to sex again.' Her eyes gleamed and his mouth curved into a sardonic smile.

'You have the two so neatly separated in your head. Do you not know that sex can be an expression of love?'

Oh, yes, she knew that. Suddenly breathlessly aware of his body close to hers, she felt her heart stop. In the two weeks they'd spent together he hadn't once touched her. But it had been there between them all the time. Simmering passion. He was biding his time and she knew it. And she had to admit that the slow build of anticipation had only added to her own excitement.

Never could she have imagined that it was possible to want a man as much as she wanted him.

He lounged by the fire next to her and her gaze was drawn to his lean, muscular legs and upwards to his broad shoulders. He had a powerfully athletic physique and suddenly she knew that if he chose to touch her now she wouldn't be able to resist him. He was the one. The only man she would ever love. The only man she would ever want. Like Nadia, she knew she would never be able to be with another.

And something had changed between them over the past two weeks.

He was gradually opening up to her. Revealing parts of himself that he'd kept carefully hidden. Confiding in her, even though she could tell that it was difficult for him. Would he do that if he felt nothing? Would he do that if all he cared about were sex?

Aware that he was watching her with those disturbing dark eyes, she scraped her hair away from her eyes and gave him a self-conscious smile.

'Where are we going tomorrow?'

His gaze didn't shift from hers and he didn't hesitate. 'To the Caves of Zatua. Time to indulge your passion for our legend, *laeela*.'

'I haven't been there for five years.'

'Then we must hope the trip lives up to your romantic expectations.'

There was something in his lazy drawl that made her look at him searchingly but there were no clues to be found in his slightly amused gaze.

Was it coincidence that he'd chosen to take her there at the end of the promised two weeks? She wanted to ask whether they'd be on their own, but she wasn't sure whether she wanted that to be the case. In fact, she didn't know what she wanted anymore. Her resolve to stay away from him had been weakened by their growing intimacy and the slow throb of unfulfilled passion that grew stronger each day.

She didn't know what she wanted anymore, but it was time to decide because she knew that a man like Tariq wouldn't be prepared to wait much longer.

Tariq lay by the fire long after she'd retired to bed.

What, he wondered to himself, *had come over him*? Never before had he felt even the smallest desire to discuss his past with a woman, let alone a woman that he intended to divorce a mere forty days after the wedding.

He wasn't the confiding type—had never felt the need to spill his guts to anyone, man or woman. It wasn't his style and never had been. From childhood he'd been taught to control and contain his emotions, and that was what he'd always done.

So why had he just spent a long evening telling Farrah Tyndall things about himself that even his closest advisers didn't know?

He'd even talked about his mother and that was something that he'd *never* been driven to do before.

With a soft curse he ran a hand over the back of his neck and put his uncharacteristic behaviour down to physical frustration. He saw her on a daily basis but he'd made a strategic decision not to touch her. To give her the space she so obviously thought she needed. He was not accustomed to exercising such self-denial but, on this occasion, he was willing to do whatever it took to bring this deal to a successful conclusion.

And the strangest thing of all was that he'd actually found himself enjoying her company on their lengthy trips together. She'd shown herself to be surprisingly intelligent and well informed.

But, he reminded himself quickly, that was only because he'd removed all opportunity for her to indulge her party habit.

Given the right set of circumstances, he had no doubt that Farrah Tyndall would revert to type and become the shallow socialite again. It was fortunate that he had plans for curbing her addiction to the empty lifestyle that she enjoyed so much. He'd decided to make the most of their limited time together. For the short duration of their marriage she would remain confined to his bed.

After two frustratingly long weeks of unnatural celibacy, letting her walk away untouched had tested his control to its limits but he told himself that it was only for one more night.

Everything was in place. Everything was arranged.

He'd given her two weeks to make up her mind and the two weeks was up tomorrow.

Tomorrow she would be his.

Their marriage would take place. The shares would be his.

And after forty days and forty nights he would divorce her.

They left at lunchtime, driving across the dusty sun-baked dunes towards the Caves of Zatua.

Farrah sat in silence, painfully aware of the feverish tension that was building between them. He was so close and she was aware of every move he made. Ignoring him had become impossible. What was it about this man that made it so difficult to breathe? Why was it that she couldn't look at him and not think about sex? She wasn't like that and never had been. She had plenty of male friends and she never *once* thought about sex in their company. With Tariq it seemed she could think about nothing else.

The attraction she felt was becoming almost intolerable. It was hard to be in such a confined space and not reach for him. She wanted to slide her hands through that luxuriant black hair, run her fingers along his roughened jaw and sink her teeth into his bronzed muscular shoulder. She wanted to strip his clothes off and see him naked! And yet not once during the fortnight they'd just spent together had he made a move in her direction.

After that first steamy kiss in the car on the way to the camp—a kiss that had been merely a manoeuvre on his part— he hadn't made a single sexual overture.

They'd talked, he'd taken her on endless trips and they'd eaten meals together. Occasionally his hand lingered on hers a moment longer than was strictly necessary and sometimes she caught him looking at her with that deadly gleam in his eyes. But he hadn't kissed her again.

And yet neither of them could fail to be aware that the fortnight that he'd promised was now complete. Today was the last day.

When was he going to ask her for her decision?

And what was her decision going to be?

As she walked towards the entrance of the caves she thought of Nadia. Was this how she had felt before she'd plunged into her passionate affair with the Sultan? Had she had doubts or had love and passion swept away common sense?

In his usual decisive fashion, Tariq grasped her hand, his long strong fingers closing over hers.

'Come.' It was a command and she followed his lead,

walking next to him into the huge cavern that guarded the entrance to the labyrinth of caves.

The first cavern was alight with flickering candles and intricately woven rugs had been placed on the ground. Tariq glanced around him with satisfaction.

Everything had been carried out exactly as he'd instructed.

He heard her shocked, delighted gasp and knew that the effort on his part had produced the desired response.

She turned to him, her gaze a mixture of delight and confusion. 'It's so beautiful,' she breathed. 'Who did this?'

'I did. I'm trying to demonstrate that I'm capable of romance.' His smile held a hint of wry self-mockery. 'You've always loved these caves. They mean a great deal to you, which is why I have chosen to bring you here to ask you the question that has been on both our minds for the past two weeks. Marry me, Farrah.' He watched with satisfaction as the breath left her body in a soft rush.

'That sounded more like a command than a question.' She lifted a hand and placed it on the centre of his chest, her touch light and teasing.

'I want you as my wife. I've been patient for two weeks. Now I need to hear your answer. If the answer is yes, then you will marry me here.'

She stilled, a flare of shock lighting her green eyes. 'You want to marry me here? Now? In the caves?'

'What better place than where Nadia and her Sultan first discovered their love and where we too first discovered our feelings for each other?'

The thoughtful silence that greeted his words was not what he had expected. He felt his tension levels soar, although why that should be the case escaped him. He was a man who positively thrived on complex business negotiations. The safe and the predictable bored him. He preferred the impossible to the possible. Having reminded himself of the facts, he waited for the usual adrenaline buzz that accompanied the climax of each major deal. Instead he felt something more akin to—panic?

He dismissed the thought instantly, reminding himself of the far-reaching implications of failing to close this particular deal. It was natural that her answer should take on greater than average importance, he assured himself.

Determined to sway her decision, Tariq slid an arm round her waist and clamped her against him. 'Say yes. And say it quickly,' he commanded. 'My patience is running out.'

'What patience is that? It seems to me that whenever you want something, you just dish out orders and it happens.'

'So I know what I want and I go after it. What's wrong with that?' He gave an arrogant lift of his head, deciding that he'd had enough of tiptoeing round the edges. 'I want you in my bed and in my life. And I have shown a great deal of patience up until this point. No other woman has *ever* made me wait the way you have made me wait.'

And he'd had enough of waiting. Staring down into her soft green eyes, he felt lust spear his body. She was exquisite and really he was to be congratulated for having waited this long.

She raised an eyebrow. 'Learning to wait for something has probably been good for your emotional development.'

'My emotions are in excellent health, thank you,' he groaned, lowering his head and kissing her neck. *She smelt of paradise.* 'I'd be grateful for an answer any time you feel ready to give it. Just make sure it's in the next three seconds.'

'I feel as though I'm standing on the top of one of your highest sand dunes,' she confessed in a soft voice. 'I don't know whether to step back and opt for safety or whether to plunge forward and risk the danger of falling.'

His eyes gleamed. 'Life with no danger becomes nothing more than an existence. Danger is what makes the miracle of life so precious, *laeela*. Only when you take risks can you know what it is like to truly live.'

'Spoken like a devotee of extreme sports,' she said dryly. 'Before I give you my answer, I need to ask you one question, Tariq.' She stared up at him, a strange light in her eyes. 'And I need you to answer honestly.'

Immediately on the defensive, Tariq racked his brains in an attempt to work out if he'd overlooked something. If he had, then it was going to be difficult to provide it at this late stage. 'Ask your question.'

She hesitated, almost as if she were afraid to voice what was in her head. 'Why do you want to marry me?'

He relaxed. 'That's easy—' He gave a confident smile. 'You're beautiful, you're good company, I enjoy talking to you and you amuse me. I even like the way you speak without any attempt at censorship—' He broke off, astonished at the length of the list and by the fact that the question had been so easy to answer.

'What you've described is friendship, Tariq.'

He frowned, wondering why she wasn't as impressed by the length of the list as he was. 'And shouldn't a good marriage be about friendship?'

It was more than his own parents had ever had, he thought bitterly.

'Of course, but there has to be more than friendship.'

Deciding that physical contact was called for, Tariq gave a smile and pulled her firmly into his arms. 'Of course there is more to marriage than friendship. There is also an amazing attraction between us.' He slid his hands over the rounded curve of her bottom, mentally applauding himself for having displayed such uncharacteristic self-control up until this point. In view of his restraint, it was surely impossible for her to misinterpret his intentions. 'That goes without saying.'

She pushed at his chest, trying to hold him at a distance. 'That's sex, Tariq. So far you've mentioned friendship and sex.

Neither of those are reasons to get married. The most important ingredient is missing.'

Alarm bells rang in his head.

It was obvious what she believed the missing ingredient to be.

Like a cornered lion, Tariq felt rising apprehension and discomfort. That feeling of panic took him by the throat. It was clear to him that she wanted him to say, *I love you.* Every muscle in his body tensed and a sheen of sweat broke out on his brow as he steeled himself to say the three words he'd spent his entire life avoiding.

Still trying to circumvent the issue, his mind quickly ran through a few possible alternatives. *You're very beautiful. I want you in my bed. You're good company.*

He'd already tried all those and *still* she wasn't satisfied. One glance at the expectation in her shining eyes was sufficient to convince him that substitute words were not going to suffice.

He took a deep breath and licked his lips. How hard could it be?

'You're an amazing woman—'

'Thank you.' Her eyes gleamed with ironic humour. 'I'm glad you think so, but it isn't a reason to marry.'

Was she doing this intentionally to torture him? 'I—' He ran a hand over the back of his neck and she gave a soft laugh and wrapped her arms round his neck, her eyes dancing, her smile warm and trusting.

'Just three little words, Tariq. How hard can it be?'

Very hard, as he was fast discovering. He stiffened and steeled himself to make the effort that was so obviously required of him but she hugged him tightly and stood on tiptoe to kiss his cheek.

'You've never said those words to anyone before, have you, Tariq?'

He shook his head, his eyes wary. She was smiling. *Why was she smiling?*

'I know you love me.' She said the words quietly. 'But I'm going to need to hear you say it. Often. So you're going to have to practice. And yes, I'll marry you.'

She knew he loved her? How?

He was so busy wondering exactly *which* part of his behaviour had suggested to her that he was in love that it took him a few moments to realize that she'd given him the answer he'd been waiting for.

'You will marry me?' The degree of pleasure he experienced at her words surprised and unsettled him. But then he reminded himself that this marriage was the final part of an important business deal on his part. A deal that had proved far more complex than he'd anticipated. Of course he had every right to be pleased. He would take over her father's company. The pipeline could be built. The future of Tazkash was secure. 'You're saying yes?'

'I'm saying yes because you've finally proved that you understand me,' she said softly, her expression dreamy as she looked up at him. 'You didn't arrange for some enormous formal wedding with loads of boring guests. You arranged this—' She waved a hand around the illuminated cave. 'And this is the most romantic thing you could have done. It's just you and me. It's about the two of us and no one else. And that's how I know you love me.'

Slightly stunned at her interpretation of what he'd considered to be no more than an elaborate business plan, Tariq smiled. 'Obviously we need someone to marry us and witnesses—'

'And, knowing you, there are several of your staff waiting at this moment to receive your call.'

'How do you know that?'

'Because you're a very controlling personality,' she teased, 'and I know you wouldn't have set this up without having thought of everything.'

He found the fact that someone knew him that well vaguely

disconcerting. Never before had he gained the impression that women had even the remotest understanding of the workings of the male sex. Farrah was proving to be disturbingly astute.

'So—' she glanced down at herself with a rueful smile, '—did you think of clothing, or am I getting married in my jeans?'

'Yasmina has brought you a dress.'

'Good.' She reached up and kissed him. 'So let's get on with it, shall we?'

CHAPTER SEVEN

FARRAH stood in her wedding dress, trying to remember a moment in her life when she'd felt happier.

She'd just married the man that she loved in a place that had always been special to her. And it had been *incredibly* romantic.

Vows had been exchanged in front of witnesses. She was wearing his ring.

It was hard to see how life could be better.

Overwhelmed with happiness, she turned to Tariq and hugged him tightly. 'I love you so much.' His powerful frame went rigid in response to her unguarded declaration and she felt his immediate withdrawal. Pulling away slightly, she tipped her head back so that she could see his face. Thick dark lashes shielded the expression in his eyes but his mouth was hard and unsmiling. She felt a sudden flash of uncertainty. And insecurity. 'It makes you uncomfortable, doesn't it, when I hug you?'

His hesitation was barely perceptible. 'It's not a problem. You may hug me if you wish. I understand that women have a greater need for affection than men.'

As answers went, it wasn't entirely reassuring. 'I don't think that's true. It's just that men aren't always comfortable with their emotions.'

But she was going to make him comfortable, she decided. She was going to make him open up and confide in her.

He studied her, a curious expression in his eyes. 'I've never met anyone quite like you before,' he confessed, his voice slightly unsteady. 'You're very affectionate. You don't hold anything back. You don't hide anything.'

She felt a sharp pang of guilt, aware that there was a *huge* part of herself that she was hiding. Concealing her true self had become second nature to her, so much so that even now, when everything had changed between them, she couldn't quite bring herself reveal the person she really was.

Anyway, what was the hurry? Tariq needed a wife who was prepared to socialize. He didn't want or need to hear that it wasn't her favourite pastime. Hadn't he approached her a second time because she'd shown that she was capable of holding her own on the social scene that he frequented?

She smiled, thinking that part of the fun of their marriage would be making discoveries about each other. 'I certainly think it's important to tell someone that you love them.'

And if she was a little disappointed that he still hadn't said those words to her, she pushed the emotion away. After everything he'd told her about his childhood, was it really surprising that he had trouble showing his emotions? They were difficult words to say if you'd never been encouraged to say them, and clearly Tariq had never been allowed to express his emotions in any way. She'd be wrong to expect too much of him too quickly.

She understood only too well the impact that one's upbringing could have on behaviour.

Food was served against the backdrop of the setting sun, but Farrah found it hard to eat anything at all. Her nerves were jumping and her stomach was churning and she was breathlessly aware of Tariq, lounging on the rug right next to her.

He was as much at home here in the desert as he was in his palace, she thought, watching as he selected various delicacies and placed them on her plate.

'You're not eating, *laeela*.' His voice was low and seductive and his eyes swept her face in question. 'You have lost your appetite?'

The way he looked at her sent a jolt of awareness through her body and she managed a shaky smile. 'I'm not that hungry.' They were surrounded by a discreet army of staff and yet it was as if they were alone.

Casting a final lingering glance in her direction, Tariq rose to his feet in a smooth athletic movement and dismissed the staff with an imperious wave of his bronzed hand.

'Why are you sending them away?' Farrah watched in surprise as the staff melted away to the Jeeps. 'We still have to drive back to the camp.'

'Not tonight.' He drew her to her feet, very much in command of the situation. 'Tonight we stay in the caves.'

'Here?' She looked up at his arrogant, proud features and her heart thudded against her chest. 'We're *sleeping* in the cave?'

His answering smile was both seductive and dangerous. 'I don't anticipate much sleeping, *laeela,* but yes, we are spending the night in the cave. Like Nadia and her Sultan.'

As she watched the last of the convoy pull away from the caves Farrah licked her lips and her eyes slid back to his. 'On our own?'

His eyes held a hint of mockery. 'For what I have in mind, I don't require an audience.'

Her pulse rate surged at an alarming rate. 'I can't believe you've arranged this—'

'Despite what you say about me, I am trying to understand you. You grew up dreaming of Nadia and her Sultan, together in this cave. Their relationship was the centre of all your childish fantasies.' His voice was husky and he lifted a hand and withdrew the pins from her hair, allowing it to fall unrestrained around her shoulders. 'And I am more than prepared to indulge your fantasies.'

'Tariq—'

His hand tightened over hers and he led her along the narrow passageway that led through the rocks to the second cave. Again it was lit with candles and the rugs were strewn with cushions and velvet throws. The atmosphere was seductive and intimate.

'Oh—' She stared in amazement. 'You planned all this?'

'Of course. I remembered that you didn't like the dark when we first came here five years ago. And now that is definitely enough talking. For two whole weeks we have done nothing but talk.' He groaned and hauled her against him in a decisive movement. 'Have you *any* idea how long I've been waiting to undress you?'

Her stomach flipped over with nerves. 'You married me just so that you can undress me?'

'I was getting to the point where I would have done almost anything in order to win the right to undress you,' he confessed unsteadily, his arm anchored firmly around her hips.

Held against his hard, muscular strength she felt her limbs weaken. 'Are we going to blow out the candles?'

'No. Definitely not. I want to see all of you.' His voice was husky as he trailed burning kisses down her neck. 'I want to see your face when I finally make love to you.'

His words sent a wicked thrill through her body. 'Tariq—'

'I have *never* wanted a woman as much as I want you—'

Breathless and trembling with anticipation, she told herself that it didn't matter that he couldn't actually bring himself to say the words she wanted to hear so badly. He'd married her and the ceremony had been full of romantic gestures. He'd *shown* her that he loved her. That was enough. Finally she'd met a man who loved *her*, rather than her money or her father's influence. In time she'd teach him how to be comfortable with his emotions.

'You haven't touched me for the past fortnight—'

'Because I didn't want you accusing me of only wanting you for sex,' he muttered as his mouth hovered over hers. 'I've taken so many cold showers that my staff are beginning to question my sanity. And I've been trying so hard to understand you that my brain is aching.'

He slid a hand into her hair and tilted her head back to allow him better access. His mouth was close, so *close*, and the heat and anticipation built inside her.

She'd waited so long for this moment. She'd imagined, she'd dreamed—

'So—' He raked his fingers through her long hair, his gaze hungry as he scanned her face. 'What did the Sultan do next, do you think, *laeela*?'

Her heart pounded against her ribs. 'I expect he undressed her slowly.'

'Slowly?' One ebony brow lifted and there was a sardonic gleam in his eyes. 'In that case I think we could have hit our first problem.' His gaze holding hers, he released her and stepped back. Then he reached inside his robes, withdrew a dagger and with a swift, precise movement of the deadly blade he cut her dress from neck to waist.

The priceless white silk slithered into a pool at her feet and she gave a gasp of shock. 'Tariq—'

He tossed the dagger casually to one side and gave an apologetic shrug of his broad shoulders. 'It is entirely possible that I'm not as patient as your Sultan,' he confessed in a regretful tone that held more humour than sincerity. 'Where you're concerned, I don't do "slow". I've waited five years for this moment and that is long enough.' His eyes glowed dark with purpose and her breath caught in her throat.

What woman could fail to be flattered by the burning need she saw in his gaze? What woman could fail to feel powerful and feminine when on the receiving end of such a blatantly sexual appraisal?

He wanted her. *He wanted her so much that he couldn't even be bothered with a few buttons.*

Tariq muttered something unintelligible under his breath and then shed his robes in a few smooth movements. Totally unselfconscious and with his usual arrogance, he swept her high in his arms and lowered her gently on to the piled cushions, his eyes fixed on hers.

'At last, you are mine—' The words were a clear statement of possession and she gave a shiver of longing.

'Kiss me,' she breathed against his mouth, the excitement inside her building to breaking point, '*please kiss me—*'

And he did.

'I'm going to discover you piece by piece.' His mouth was hot and demanding, the skilled and subtle probe of his tongue an erotic and intimate prelude to what was to follow. The chemistry between them exploded with frightening force. She felt breathless and dizzy, as though she were poised on the edge of something dangerous, *something that would change her for ever*, and instinctively her arms slid round his neck, seeking his protection.

The flickering candles provided just enough light for her to see the harsh planes of his handsome face, for her to make out the burning intent glowing in his eyes.

He shifted slightly, covering her with his lean, powerful frame as his mouth took hers. His kiss was possessive and urgent and she was breathlessly aware of the hard heat of his body. She arched in an involuntary movement, hearing his groan of approval as he lifted his mouth from hers and transferred his attention to her breasts.

The skilled flick of his tongue over her nipple sent sharp stabs of sensation shooting low in her pelvis and she pressed against him in an instinctive attempt to soothe the throbbing ache that was building within her body.

It was only as she felt the cool air of the cave whisper over her bare skin that she realized that he'd somehow removed the last of her clothing. She was naked under him and she felt the leisurely, seductive stroke of his hand over her thigh.

'I'm going to torture you with pleasure,' he promised in husky tones and proceeded to do just that. He kissed and caressed every part of her body except that one most intimate place that ached to be touched. He licked the top of her thigh, dragged slow kisses over her stomach, always withholding what she wanted most. She shifted and moved and the ache inside her intensified until it was almost pain and desperation rose to screaming pitch.

Did he know? she wondered. Did he have any idea what he was doing to her?

And then he lifted his head and she saw the wicked self-satisfied gleam in his eyes.

He knew.

'Tariq, please—' Losing all her inhibitions, she reached for him, her fingers touching him intimately for the first time. She gave a violent shiver of excitement as she felt the power of his aroused manhood, registered his size with a flicker of trepidation. But, before she could think, he reached down and finally touched her where she was longing to be touched.

Sensation merged and mingled until she could no longer distinguish exactly what he was doing to her. His fingers moved with skill and awareness as he touched and teased until her entire focus was on the incessant, blinding ache deep inside her.

Everything went from her head except the desperate need for him. She wrapped her legs around his waist, urging him on with her body and he slipped an arm under her hips and raised her.

'Look at me—' His command was hoarse and urgent and her eyes flew wide with shock and breathless abandon as he entered her with a purposeful thrust that joined them in the most intimate way possible.

Shocked by the size of him, her body instinctively tightened and she felt him pause, his eyes darkening as he stared down at her. 'Farrah?'

'Don't stop! Oh, please, don't stop now,' she groaned and

he drew in an unsteady breath and moved again, but this time more gently.

Sensation flashed and exploded and she gave a gasp of pleasure that he misinterpreted.

'I don't want to hurt you—' He looked strangely uncertain and she shook her head.

'You're not—please, Tariq. I need—I want—' She broke off and closed her eyes, unable to verbalize exactly what it was that she wanted but hoping that he could make the necessary translation.

He did.

He moved again and the feelings in her body escalated until every thought in her head was eclipsed by a sensation so wild and all consuming that she could do no more than cry out his name and move in the way that he urged her to move as he guided them both towards sexual oblivion.

When the explosion came it took them both together in a shower of sensation so intense that she clutched at him as if he was the only one that could save her from the madness.

And perhaps he felt it too because he drove into her hard and then held her against him, murmuring something against her neck while his body throbbed into hers.

Tariq lay in the dark with Farrah wrapped around him. Her head was on his chest, strands of blond hair were spread over his arm and the cushions beneath them and her limbs were tangled with his. Listening to her peaceful steady breathing, he knew that she slept.

In the aftermath of the most incredible sex of his life he was being forced to re-evaluate almost all his preconceived ideas about marriage. He was shocked to discover that he actually enjoyed the idea that she belonged to him and no one else. And the biggest shock of all was the discovery that she'd been a virgin.

It was true that the file on her that currently lay in his desk contained no evidence of her involvement with a man, but never, not once, had it crossed his mind that she might be innocent.

The knowledge that he'd been the first and only man to experience the seductive passion of Farrah Tyndall brought a soft smile of masculine satisfaction to his face. But the smile faded the instant he remembered that in forty days and forty nights he would release her from the bonds of matrimony, which would leave her free to link up with any man of her choosing.

And, given the degree of male adulation she'd received when she'd strolled on to the catwalk, she wasn't going to find any shortage of willing candidates.

At the mere thought of Farrah with another man he was suddenly filled with a possessiveness so intense that he contemplated creating a landslide that would trap them in the cave for ever.

He had no intention of *ever* sharing her with *anyone*.

Which left him facing a situation he hadn't anticipated.

He'd entertained the idea of marriage only because he knew that it would be short-lived. The fact that he might not want to divorce her at the end of forty days and forty nights hadn't crossed his mind.

Why would it? Farrah Tyndall was no one's idea of good wife material. She was flighty and shallow and her priorities were all wrong. It would be impossible for him to persuade his people to take a woman like her to their hearts. The marriage had been no more than a business deal designed to give him ownership of her shares.

He'd married her only because he knew that divorce would follow.

And yet why would he even contemplate ending something which had brought him the greatest pleasure he'd ever experienced?

The solution was simple, he decided, tightening his grip on her soft, curvaceous body. He wouldn't divorce her. They would remain married.

Instead of taking over the company, he would work in partnership with her father to build the pipeline. He had no doubt that, now that he'd actually married Farrah, Harrison Tyndall would be prepared to reopen negotiations. She need never know that the company was his original reason for marrying her.

And, as for her unfortunate partying habit—he frowned slightly as he searched for a solution. She was surprisingly intelligent and she'd coped well with life in the desert. He just needed to make sure that she was kept well away from charity balls and fashion shows. If he kept her on a tight leash and watched her every move in public, could it not work?

Of course it could. All he had to do was to arrange for her to have an extensive staff to watch her every move when he wasn't around to do so himself.

With that in place, she could stay as his wife and his plan to divorce her would stay well and truly buried.

Why risk upsetting her unnecessarily when that situation was now in the past?

Having found a satisfactory solution designed to keep her by his side for ever, he slid a hand down the smooth skin of her back and decided that she'd *definitely* slept for quite long enough…

Farrah woke feeling deliciously warm. Her body ached in unusual places and she was instantly aware of Tariq's arms holding her securely against him.

The memories of the intimacies they'd shared during the night brought a touch of colour to her cheeks and she lifted her head with a shy smile.

'Have I told you that I love you and that I think you're incredible?'

His dark eyes locked with hers and flashed with fierce determination. 'You are mine and you're staying that way,' he said decisively and she frowned slightly, wondering why he felt the need to say that after they'd been through a marriage ceremony. *Of course she was his.*

She pressed a lingering kiss on his bronzed shoulder. 'You're possessive, do you know that? Domineering, controlling and overprotective.'

His arms tightened around her. 'Never before,' he said huskily, 'but with you, yes. I have discovered the meaning of all those words. You are mine, always, for ever.'

Basking in a warm haze of masculine appreciation, Farrah lay back and watched as tiny fingers of light found their way into the cave. 'I don't ever want to leave here,' she whispered softly. 'It's perfect here.'

Tariq tensed. 'It *is* perfect, but sadly we cannot spend the rest of our lives in this cave.'

'How about the rest of the day?'

'Not even that, I'm afraid.'

'What's happened to your controlling, demanding personality? You're the Sultan. Everyone has to obey you.' She rolled on top of him, blond hair tangling with dark. 'You can tell everyone that this is where you're going to live from now on. They can drop off food parcels.'

He reached up and pushed her hair away from her face, his expression fierce. 'It is what we share that matters, *laeela,* not where we choose to share it.'

'Oh—' Her heart skipped and danced and she lowered her head and kissed him. 'That's the most romantic thing anyone has ever said to me. And, just for that, I'll forgive you for saying we have to leave. Are we going back to Nazaar?'

'Not to Nazaar.'

Something about the way he was looking at her made her suddenly anxious and she drew back slightly. 'Where, then? Where are we going?'

'We have to return to Fallouk.'

Fallouk.

The word made an ugly dent in the smooth, warm atmosphere. Farrah sat upright, blond hair sliding over her shoulders, horror on her face. 'No.'

'It was inevitable that we would have to return there.' His tone was level. Unemotional. 'It is my home. And my home is now your home.'

'We can't go there, not yet.' Her own tone was frantic and clogged with emotion. 'That was where everything went wrong last time.'

'Things will not go wrong this time,' he assured her immediately, reaching out and pulling her back into his arms. 'You are my wife and no one can change that.'

It was true, she assured herself as she relaxed against him and tried to make the most of their last moments together in the cave. She *was* his wife. But even that knowledge couldn't dispel the sick feeling of unease that rose inside her.

Farrah sat silent in the back of the chauffeur-driven car, her feeling of foreboding growing stronger with every mile they drew closer to the capital city and the Palace.

As if to match her dark mood, thunder and lightning flashed through the sky and she stared into the deepening gloom wondering if the worsening weather was an omen. A portent of things to come?

Telling herself that she was being ridiculous she tried to forget, but instead she found herself remembering every minute detail of her last visit to Fallouk, the ancient capital city of Tazkash...

After a month living in the desert camp at Nazaar, Tariq's father's ill health dictated that they all return to the capital city. Tariq insisted that she return with him.

Madly in love, convinced that it was only a matter of time before he proposed, Farrah readily agreed but found herself more than a little daunted by the opulence and formality of palace life.

The truth was, to the constant chagrin of her sociable mother, she wasn't comfortable at glitzy parties and functions.

'I don't know what to do or what to say,' she'd confessed to Tariq a few days later but he'd brushed her fears aside, suddenly remote and distracted and nothing like the man whose company she'd enjoyed so much during their time in the desert.

'Any of my family will help you,' he'd assured her with a faint frown. 'If you have questions, you only have to ask.'

She wondered if she ought to point out that, after the initial introductions to endless cousins, uncles and aunts, none of his family had come near her. She'd spent the last few days on her own in her room, reading.

'I hardly see you—'

'My father is unwell. I have urgent matters of state to attend to—'

She smiled, feeling horribly guilty for being the one to put extra pressure on him. 'Of course, I'm sorry—don't worry, I'll be fine.'

'There is a formal dinner tonight—' Distracted and unusually tense, his eyes flickered to one of his advisers who hovered anxiously at a discreet distance, obviously eager to escort him to yet another meeting. 'I will arrange for someone to help you prepare.'

And from then on it had been downhill all the way.

Racked by insecurities and longing for just five minutes alone with him so she could ask him some questions about how she should be dressing and behaving, Farrah spent ages selecting something suitable to wear for her first formal dinner.

Finally satisfied with her choice, she was just adding some discreet jewellery when a young woman strolled into her room.

'I'm Asma, Tariq's cousin. He asked me to come and help you dress.' Her faintly superior air and slightly mocking smile suggested that it was the last job in the world she would have chosen. 'Oh—' She ran her eyes over Farrah's slim frame and pulled a face.

Already lacking in confidence, Farrah bit her lip. 'Something's wrong with the way I'm dressed?'

His cousin opened her mouth and then closed it again with a faint smile. 'Not at all. You look delightful.'

Farrah glanced down at herself. She'd chosen the dress so carefully. 'I thought it was discreet.' Determined to get it right, she'd chosen to wear long sleeves and a high neck. 'I want to make the right impression.' She didn't dare admit that she didn't even enjoy formal functions that much.

'Of course you do. But Tariq is a man used to being with *extremely* beautiful women. You're never going to hold him if you dress like a nun,' Asma murmured, her huge dark eyes roving over Farrah with something approaching pity. 'My cousin appreciates beautiful women.'

Farrah bit her lip. The cruel reminder of Tariq's reputation with her sex made her stomach sink and all her youthful insecurities rush to the surface.

Why would he possibly be interested in her? He mixed with sophisticated mature women who knew exactly what games to play to keep him ensnared and interested. Whereas she—

She caught a glimpse of herself in the mirror and let out a sigh of frustration.

She was just a girl and it showed. She laughed at the wrong times, talked at the wrong times and dressed in the wrong clothes. Her own mother had despaired of her. What could a man like Tariq possibly see in her?

In the desert she'd felt that they'd connected, but here—here amongst the splendour and the formality she felt totally out of her depth.

But then she remembered the kiss they'd shared at the caves of Zatua. He loved her, she knew he did. And she would learn everything there was to know about palace life, she told herself with a determined lift of her chin. She could *learn* to be the sort of wife he needed and wanted.

'All right—' Turning away from the mirror, she started to unzip her dress. 'Tell me what I should be wearing, Asma. I need your help.' Instinctively trusting, she turned to the other girl for advice.

'Something short and low-cut,' Asma said immediately, reaching for something from the rail. 'This looks good.'

It looked like something her mother would have chosen. Farrah looked at it doubtfully. 'I wouldn't normally wear anything that revealing.'

'But do you normally date guys like Tariq?' Asma's smile did little to conceal her disbelief at her cousin's current choice. 'He dates the most sophisticated women in the world—princesses, actresses, models—'

'All right, thanks, I'll try it.' Farrah interrupted her hastily, not wanting to hear any more about the type of woman Tariq usually chose. Her confidence was at an all-time low and she didn't need the fact that she was an unusual choice for him battered home by a member of his family.

He was single, wasn't he? So obviously he'd never been in love before now. And that, she told herself firmly as she wriggled into a dress that made her blush, was the difference between her and the competition.

She stared at herself doubtfully in the mirror and tugged the neckline upwards. 'You're sure this is suitable?'

'Absolutely,' Asma replied smoothly. 'I think we can safely say that if you wear this tonight Tariq won't be able to take his eyes off you.'

Her prediction proved to be correct, but not for the reasons that Farrah had assumed. Far from being dazzled by her beauty and glamour, Tariq had looked at her with a frowning disapproval that he hadn't attempted to conceal.

'That dress is *not* suitable. You should have asked my family for advice on how to dress,' he said coldly and she gritted her teeth, ignoring the sting of tears behind her eyes, trying not to feel hurt at his complete lack of understanding.

And, as for Asma—she realized, too late, that the girl clearly had her own agenda, but she was nowhere to be seen and Farrah was forced to endure a hideous evening, aware that she'd committed an enormous social *faux pas* and had embarrassed Tariq as well as herself.

Why Asma had chosen to put her in this position was a mystery to her.

Furious with herself for being so naïve and trusting and feeling miserably self-conscious amongst the formally dressed women, Farrah picked at her food and kept her mouth shut, afraid to risk expressing an opinion. She'd already put her foot in it. She didn't want to risk making another mistake. She didn't want to draw attention to herself. And she was just mortified at having been so gullible and not having followed her own instincts when it came to matters of dress.

As a result of her own desperate embarrassment, she met all Tariq's attempts to converse with monosyllabic answers and tried not to mind when he finally gave up and started to talk to the beautiful redhead seated to his right.

As far as she was concerned, the evening couldn't end soon enough and she escaped back to her room at the earliest opportunity.

He sought her out the following morning. 'You should have asked for advice on what to wear. I will arrange for one of my aunts to talk to you.'

'If she's related to Asma then please don't bother,' Farrah muttered, trying not to sound sulky. 'I think I've just about had all the help I can stand from your family.'

His gaze was chilly. 'What is that supposed to mean?'

'Well, they're not exactly welcoming, are they? It is perfectly obvious that they don't want me here. They resent me.' Asma had blatantly set out to embarrass and humiliate her in front of Tariq.

'That's nonsense.' His brows came together in a frown. 'Why would they resent you?'

'I have no idea,' she said flatly. 'Unlike you, I don't have a PhD in palace politics.' She looked at his rigid profile and suddenly the fight drained out of her. 'Don't let's argue. I love you, Tariq.'

His gaze softened slightly. 'Things have not been easy since we arrived here, I understand that. There is something I have to ask you and perhaps this is a good time.'

Her heart suddenly skipped and danced. The humiliation of the previous evening was forgotten as excitement took its place. This was the moment she'd been waiting for. This was the moment that Tariq was going to ask her to marry him.

Poised to say yes, she held her breath and waited expectantly.

He took her hand in his and lifted it to his mouth in a strangely old fashioned gesture. 'I suppose things are more difficult because people are unsure of why you are here. Your role hasn't yet been defined.'

She couldn't hold back the smile. *It was now.* He was going to ask her now. 'I'm sure you're right—' She'd never known such happiness. She wanted the delicious sense of anticipation to last for ever.

'So you will move into my apartment today. I'll announce it straight away. It was foolish of me to delay.' He slid an arm round her waist and dropped a lingering kiss on her mouth. 'After all, you are perfect mistress material.'

Her happiness died a dramatic and rapid death. 'Perfect mistress material?'

'Of course.' He smiled, supremely confident. 'To wait any longer would be madness given the powerful chemistry between us.'

'Perfect mistress material?' It was such a shock that she had trouble getting her tongue round the words and she stared at him blankly. 'That's what you're planning to announce?'

'You are extremely beautiful and I find you amusing company,' he assured her. 'You can move in with me. You won't even have to appear in public much. You can just keep to my suite of rooms.'

In other words, he was ashamed of her and didn't want to display her in public, she thought miserably.

And, just like that, her dreams fell to the ground and broke into pieces.

A tight band squeezed her heart. 'Let me get this straight.' Her voice shook slightly. 'You've decided that I'm good enough to have sex with you?'

He frowned. 'I'm offering you a great deal more than that.'

Her temper started to simmer. 'What, exactly?'

'A place by my side. Access to certain aspects of palace life.'

Certain aspects. 'Until you decide that you've had enough of me.' She hid her pain behind anger. 'I'm worth more than that, Tariq.'

He released her and stepped back, his bronzed hands spread in a gesture of masculine exasperation. 'I am honouring you—'

'No, you're insulting me,' she said flatly, turning away so that she didn't have to look at him. *Wasn't tempted to just throw herself in his arms and accept him on any terms.* 'You're every bit as bad as the sultan in the legend. He was ashamed of Nadia, just as you're ashamed of me.'

'You are as dreamy and impractical as Nadia. But now we reach the truth.' His voice was silky smooth and she tensed as he strolled up behind her. 'You were expecting marriage.'

The fact that he was aware of her hopes simply added to her humiliation and she turned angrily, blinking back tears.

'I realize now that Nadia was an utter fool! Instead of killing herself, she should have killed the Sultan for being such a short-sighted, selfish *bastard*,' The word came out on a sob and he inhaled sharply.

'Our legend has twisted your thinking, but—'

'My thinking is perfectly straight, thank you,' she yelled, ignoring the fact that her voice could probably be heard halfway round the palace. She didn't care! She just couldn't believe what he was saying. She loved him. 'It's you that's twisted! You're not capable of loving anyone except yourself. All you think about is yourself.'

Proud and unyielding, he threw back his head, his dark eyes ablaze. 'You are angry because you wanted the position of my wife,' he said coldly, 'but—'

'You make it sound like a job application!' She flung the words at him like stones. 'You just don't get it, do you? Why do you think I wanted to marry you, Tariq?'

His shoulders were tense and he was very much a man on the defensive. 'For the same reason that the peasant girl wanted to marry the Sultan. For power and position.'

She turned away, not wanting to reveal the depth of her feelings. Not only did he not love her, but he didn't believe in her love for him.

The past few weeks had obviously meant nothing to him. He thought she was interested in glitz and glamour. He thought she wanted access to his lifestyle.

How could he have misunderstood her so greatly?

And how could she have been such a gullible fool?

But the answer to that was obvious. She'd been a gullible fool because she'd fallen in love with him, she told herself miserably. And love was always generous and optimistic. She'd trusted him. She'd believed in him.

And he'd proved he was a total rat.

She needed to get away fast, before she gave in to her misery and did something totally uncool like begging him...

Dragged back to the present, Farrah gave a tiny laugh. She'd been an innocent, trusting fool, she reflected. So trusting that she hadn't seen the malice in Asma. Hadn't expected even for a moment that she had been doing her best to sabotage a relationship.

But she would never have been able to have sabotaged it

without Tariq's help, she reminded herself. He'd been so willing to see the worst in her.

Suddenly everything about her had been unsuitable.

Every step she'd taken in the Palace, her foot had slid right in it up to the thigh. And in the end she'd stopped taking advice from his family because it had been so clear to her that they'd wanted her out of his life.

It would be different this time, Farrah assured herself as the convoy of vehicles gradually approached the ancient walled city of Fallouk.

This time she was arriving as his wife.

They'd spent time together. They enjoyed each other's company.

In his own way, he loved her. *She knew he loved her.*

It was just important to make sure that nothing went wrong. In a sudden panic, she put a hand on his arm. 'You need to tell me how to dress for everything. What's expected of me—'

'Calm yourself, *laeela*,' he said with an amused smile. 'I will take care of everything. There won't be a problem.'

As long as his family didn't interfere, she thought gloomily, wishing that she had his confidence.

'Aren't you worried that your family won't accept me?' she asked, just hating herself for appearing so insecure but, at the same time, needing something in the way of reassurance.

He hesitated and then turned his head away from her. 'My family will welcome this marriage.'

There was something in his tone that made her feel slightly uneasy but she decided that she must have imagined it. She was just apprehensive, which was entirely natural after what had happened on the last occasion she'd had a taste of palace life.

Her apprehension increased as she was escorted to an enormous suite of rooms that led on to a balcony. Stone arches overlooked a courtyard garden below. Feeling confined after the freedom of the desert, Farrah immediately stepped on to the balcony. A gushing fountain formed an impressive centrepiece to the pretty courtyard and exotic plants tumbled in an array of rich colours down the walls of the palace.

She turned to Tariq, who had followed her outside. 'What am I expected to do with my day?'

'You are my wife. Do as you please. During the day, when I am involved in matters of state, you can enjoy the Palace.' He cupped her face with his lean, strong hands and lowered his head to kiss her. 'You are my Queen. Go anywhere you please. Command as you please.' He surveyed her with benign amusement.

'And at night?' Her heart thumped as she stared up at him. 'What happens at night, Tariq?'

Watching the hot flare of desire in his dark eyes, she felt her limbs weaken alarmingly.

'At night you are mine and mine alone. I share you with no one,' he delivered in his usual arrogant style and she felt her heart miss a beat.

It was going to be all right, she told herself firmly as he released her with obvious reluctance and strode out of the room.

She was his wife and nothing his family did or said could change that.

What could possibly go wrong?

CHAPTER EIGHT

IN HER anxiety not to be late, Farrah dressed for dinner far too early and had time on her hands.

Deciding to spend the spare half an hour exploring the Palace, she wandered down corridors, her heels tapping on the marble floor as she admired paintings, furniture and the ornate ceilings.

She was on the point of returning to Tariq's private apartment when she heard hysterical sobs coming from a room close by.

Instinctively wanting to comfort anyone in so much obvious distress, she gave a sharp frown of concern and hurried towards the sound, pausing by the open doorway as she heard voices. Clearly someone else had had the same idea as herself.

'I hate her,' sobbed an anguished female voice. 'I hate her *so* much. I hate her perfect blond hair and her long legs. I hate her smile. But most of all I hate the fact he actually *married* her.'

'Calm down, Asma,' urged another voice. 'He may have married her but you know he doesn't love her.'

Farrah froze. It was Asma and her mother, Tariq's aunt. And they were talking about *her*. She wanted to leave, to run back down the corridor as quickly as she could, but her feet were glued to the spot. What, she wondered, had she ever done to Asma to deserve being on the receiving end of so much vitriol?

'He's married her,' Asma hiccoughed, her voice rising to a

hysterical pitch. 'Despite everything we did five years ago to make sure that she wasn't suitable, he's *married* her!'

'Be silent!' Her mother's voice was sharp. 'The marriage is nothing more than a business deal.'

Asma was sobbing quietly. 'That's rubbish. Of course it isn't a business deal. I saw her face when she arrived in his car! She's crazy about him and she always was.'

'Possibly. But she doesn't know that after forty days and forty nights,' the older woman said crisply, 'he will divorce her.'

There was a long silence, punctuated by a few sniffs as Asma tried to assimilate this latest piece of information. 'Why would he do that?'

Yes, why? Farrah wondered numbly from her position outside the doorway. *Why would he?*

Asma's mother helpfully supplied the answer. 'Because he doesn't love her. Tariq married her only for her shares in her father's company.'

'He's married her for her shares?'

'And they became his on marriage. In forty days he can and will divorce her,' came the firm reply. 'Leaving him free to marry whom he chooses.'

'Which would be me—' Asma's voice shook. 'It would be me, wouldn't it, Mother?'

Unable to hear the answer to that question because of the loud buzzing in her ears, Farrah wondered in a vague, detached way whether she might be about to pass out. There were disturbing clouds around the edge of her vision and suddenly she felt removed from reality. Tariq's aunt must have made some mistake, she thought numbly.

Tariq hadn't married her to gain possession of her shares.

He'd married her because he loved her. She knew he loved her.

But had he actually ever used those words?

Shocked and dazed, she backed away from the open door like someone in a dream and almost fell over a statue behind her.

Why would Tariq need her shares?

She needed to speak to Tariq. She needed to phone her father. *She needed to be sick.*

'Your Highness—'

Dizzy with horror, she turned and recognized the smooth, expressionless features of Hasim Akbar. She remembered him from the desert camp at Nazaar. Wasn't he one of Tariq's most senior advisers? 'I need to see Tariq,' she whispered, so badly in shock that she could barely form the words, 'and I need to see him right now.'

'His Excellency is currently involved in extremely delicate negotiations with the Kazbanian foreign minister and can't be disturbed, but I could—'

'I said, *right now*.' Something in her tone must have hinted at the gravity of the situation because Hasim gave her an anxious look, drew breath and bowed.

'If you would follow me, Your Highness.'

The walk down the marbled corridor was sufficiently long for her to examine the facts. Sufficiently long to ensure that by the time they finally reached the large double doors that led to the private audience chambers, she'd reached boiling point. The guards on either side of the door stood to attention and she eyed the swords that they wore as part of their ceremonial uniform, contemplating violence for the first time in her life. Shock had given way to anger. She felt outraged and affronted and so blisteringly angry that she wanted to kill someone.

Something of her undiluted fury must have shown in her face because Hasim shot her an uneasy look.

'I will announce you, Your Highness,' he began, but she swept past him and the guards without bothering to answer him.

She didn't need a sword, she thought grimly. The way she was feeling at the moment, she was more than capable of killing Tariq with her bare hands.

Utterly shattered by the realization that their marriage was a sham, she stalked through an outer chamber, ignoring the startled looks of those who were waiting to be given an audience with the Sultan, ignoring the confusion on the faces of the guards who were standing by the final doorway. In other circumstances she might have felt sorry for them. Clearly they had no idea whether they were supposed to stop her or not.

But at that moment the only person she felt sorry for was Tariq. He had no idea what was coming to him, she thought grimly as she pushed open the door and walked into the room, head held high. If he'd known then he would have run for the hills.

His dark glossy head was bowed over a set of papers but he looked up with a frown of irritation at her surprise entrance. Astonishment was replaced by caution. 'Something is wrong?'

'You're quick,' she said sweetly, 'very quick. I need to speak to you and I need to speak to you now.'

He threw down the pen he was holding and sat back in his chair, his expression falling a long way short of encouraging. 'Farrah, I am in the middle of negotiating a—'

'What I have to say could be said in public,' she said, working hard to keep her tone well modulated, 'and it probably should be. But in the interests of diplomacy I will allow you precisely sixty seconds to get rid of your guest and save yourself public humiliation.'

With a sharply indrawn breath, Tariq rose to his feet, his eyes never leaving hers. 'Faisel, if you will excuse me for a short time,' he said, 'we will resume this meeting very shortly. My staff would be honoured to offer you refreshment if you care to go next door.'

Clearly riveted by the scene playing out in front of him, the Kazbanian foreign minister rose to his feet, abandoned the pile of papers in front of him and slid silently out of the room.

'For your information, I hate scenes. And in particular I hate public scenes.' Tariq sat back in his chair, dark eyes glittering with anger, his long fingers drumming a steady rhythm on the polished table. 'I don't appreciate being disturbed in the middle of a meeting.'

'And I don't appreciate discovering that you married me for my father's shares. Allow me to say that I find your romantic streak less than overwhelming, Tariq.'

The atmosphere in the room changed in an instant.

'You're not making sense.' He uttered the words in a bored tone but his fingers stilled, his eyes narrowed and she could see his sharp brain shifting through the gears. It was the final confirmation that she needed.

Rat.

'Oh, I'm making perfect sense. And if you hate scenes then you married the wrong woman because I'm not prepared to stand by with my head bowed while you walk all over me.' Torn in two by the agony of his betrayal and the effort of holding on to her steadily collapsing emotions, she walked across the room and stared out of the window. Then she turned, her voice little more than a whisper. 'You bastard.'

Something flickered across his face. He had the look of a man who knew he was under attack but so far hadn't managed to identify the enemy. 'Farrah—'

'I thought you cared. This time I *really* thought you loved me. And what sort of a fool does that make me?'

He rose to his feet in a fluid movement, his hands on the table. 'We need to—'

'All those things we did together—' she lifted a hand to her forehead and rubbed '—all those things you said to me. And you didn't mean *any* of them.'

'You're being hysterical—'

'Too right I'm hysterical! Forty days and forty nights—' Her voice cracked as she gave voice to the words. 'You married me knowing that you were going to divorce me after forty days and forty nights. What sort of man does a thing like that? *What sort of scumbag gets married with the intention of divorcing his wife after six weeks?'*

He inhaled sharply but she didn't give him a chance to speak.

'Are you sure you can stand me for that long, Tariq? I can't *believe* what a fool I've been. It all makes sense to me now. I thought that getting married in a cave was a romantic gesture on your part but the truth is that you were afraid of marrying me in public in case someone gave the game away. Was that what all the candles were for? To make sure I couldn't see what I was doing? I thought that the time we spent at Nazaar was special, but you were simply doing what was necessary to get your own way, as usual. You are a ruthless, conscienceless rat and I can't believe that I actually slept with you!'

Muttering something in his own language, he moved so swiftly that she didn't see it coming until his fingers gripped the tops of her arms, until she had her back against the wall. 'That's enough! You have had your say, now it is your turn to listen.'

'I don't want to listen.'

'You *will* listen to me—'

'Why? So that you can tell me more lies?' His powerful body pressed hard against hers and she felt the familiar curl of excitement low in her stomach. The instinctive response sickened her. Even now, knowing what she knew, her body failed to recognize the man that he was. 'Face it, Tariq, there's no way you can dig yourself out of this hole. You're in so deep that even a rope and a ladder wouldn't save you now.' She tried to push him away but he planted an arm either side of her head, blocking her escape.

'I insist that you calm down and listen to me. Already I have allowed you more leeway than any other woman.'

'And that's supposed to flatter me? No other woman had the shares you needed, did they, Tariq? It's amazing what you can get away with when the stakes are high enough.' She could feel the tension pulsing through him and wondered with a flicker of alarm whether she'd gone too far.

'Listen to me,' he growled, 'or so help me I will make you and you may not like my methods.'

Eyes clashed, breath mingled and the atmosphere snapped tight around them. She had a feeling that his methods would include his mouth on hers and she wanted to avoid that at all costs.

Even after what had happened, she knew herself well enough to understand that if he kissed her she was lost.

'Speak, then. Make your excuses. Tell me it's all a lie.'

'It isn't a lie.'

The flat, simple statement sent a sharp pain through the centre of her chest, killing off the final flicker of hope that it had all been a terrible misunderstanding on her part.

'Then I truly, truly hate you and there's no excuse for what you've done,' she whispered. Her knees sagged and she would have slid into a heap on the floor if he hadn't caught her.

'I do not intend to make excuses. The pipeline project is essential for the future of Tazkash and it is my responsibility to protect that future. Since our talks with your father collapsed five years ago we have explored a number of other options but none of them are viable. If I have ownership of the company I can make it work. I *have* to make it work for the sake of my people. I bought up all the available shares, but—'

'Hold on a minute—' Her voice was little more than a whisper as she lifted a hand to stop him in mid flow. 'So, as well as using me, you're preparing to smash my father's life too? Preparing to take over a business he's spent his life building? Have you no conscience?'

He tensed. 'You are making it look bad, but—'

'I fail to see how even someone as ruthless and machiavellian as you could put gloss on this situation,' she said, trying to stop her teeth chattering. 'You were prepared to lower yourself to marry me for a few barrels of oil. No matter how many times you rephrase that, it isn't going to look good.'

'You too have gained from this marriage,' he said in a raw

tone. 'You have always had money so I understood I couldn't give you that, but now you have royal connections. There is no party list that will not contain your name. Your position as my wife will gain you access to any event that takes your fancy.'

'Don't you mean my position as your ex-wife? You don't have a *clue* about women, Tariq. And you have even less of a clue about *me*!' Thank goodness she'd never told him the truth about herself! Her shell was her protection. His firm hold on her was the only thing preventing her ignominious descent on to the smooth marble floor and perhaps he realized that because she felt his grip tighten.

'You are overwrought and your pride has been damaged, but—'

'Pride? I've just discovered that I'm married to a lump of *slime*, and you talk about pride?' She flung the words at him, mortified as she felt her voice crack with emotion. The fact that, even having spent time together, he knew so little about her depressed her utterly. 'You seem to think I want to spend my entire life at parties—'

'There is nothing wrong with that,' he assured her quickly in a smooth tone. 'Women are interested in different things than men; it's a fact of life and one that I have long since accepted. You like dressing up, you are addicted to shoes, you find fascination with make-up—' His helpful summary of what he clearly saw to be the main characteristics of her sex left her virtually speechless.

Surely by now he must have at least a vague inkling that she was more than a frivolous socialite?

'So why,' she annunciated when she'd finally recovered sufficiently for speech, 'if this is the sort of person that I am, have I just spent two happy weeks in the desert wearing hiking boots?'

'Because stilettos aren't good on sand?' There was a glimmer of humour in his dark eyes but she was too angry and upset to respond with anything other than a fierce glare.

'You think I lead this empty, useless life and you've never taken the trouble to get to know the real me.'

His expression was instantly guarded. He was a man on the spot and he knew it. 'I don't think you are useless and I've been very touched by how well you adapted to living in the desert,' he returned, his dark eyes scanning her face for a reaction to his words of praise.

'Let me ask you a question,' she said, her tone dangerously quiet. 'If I had to spend the rest of my life in the palace or in the desert, which would I choose?'

He didn't hesitate. 'Of course, the palace. Any woman would.'

'Wrong answer, Tariq.'

His brows met in an impatient frown. 'But you love parties—you spend your life at parties. It's what you do with your life—'

'You deal in stereotypes, Tariq. You've put all women into the same box and you can't even see—' She closed her eyes and shook her head.

What was the point in trying to correct him? The truth was she was so shattered by what she was hearing that she couldn't think of a single thing to say. She just wanted to curl up in a tiny ball and protect herself from any more hurt.

He didn't know her and he never would. *She wasn't going to give him that privilege.*

'You agreed to marry me so *clearly* you believed that this marriage would be advantageous to you also,' he said stiffly and she winced.

Advantageous?

They were just so different. How could she possibly have thought that this relationship would ever work?

'What's clear to me is that the inner workings of my mind are a total mystery to you. And actually they're a mystery to me too, because why I would choose to make a fool of myself over the same man twice in one lifetime I really don't understand,' she muttered and he looked at her with ill-concealed exasperation.

'Then *tell* me how you feel—'

'Sick?'

Sick that she'd been so stupid and trusting. That she'd let herself love him again. But clearly the words had meant nothing to him. And she wasn't about to remind him how open she'd been in her affections. For him marriages were all about mutual benefit. Another type of business deal.

'We are good together. Last night in the cave—' his voice became husky and he stroked her hair away from her face with a gentle hand '—it was incredible, *laeela*. And I decided then that forty days and forty nights with you would not be enough. You can relax because I will *not* be divorcing you.'

His complete lack of sensitivity triggered the burst of emotion that she'd been struggling to hold back and he stared at her with disbelief and no small degree of frustration as the tears spilled down her cheeks.

'You are making no sense whatsoever!' He jabbed his fingers into his hair. 'You are upset because you believed that I planned to divorce you and yet when I tell you that this is not the case, you start crying. Why?'

'Because I've never been more miserable in my life,' she said flatly, scrubbing her palm across her face and sniffing hard. 'You marry me to gain possession of the shares in my father's company but then you decide not to divorce me as originally planned because the sex was actually better than you expected. Forgive me for *not* being flattered, Tariq.'

Two spots of colour appeared on his perfect bone structure. 'You misinterpret everything I say—'

'I don't think so.' Needing to escape before she lost the last of her dignity, she wriggled out of his arms and walked over to the door. Only when the handle was safely under her fingers did she risk turning to look at him.

His handsome face might have been carved from stone, his powerful body tense and unmoving as he watched her. He looked like a man who had his back up against an electric fence. It was clear that he was trying to anticipate her next move and if the situation hadn't been so tragic she would have laughed. It was the first time ever that she could remember seeing Tariq unsure of himself. He didn't know what her next move was going to be.

And neither did she, she realized miserably. Even while her dignity and common sense told her to leave the room—leave him—a tiny, stupid part of her wanted to hurl herself into his arms and lie there safe and warm while he used his diplomatic skills to talk his way out of this vile situation and made it possible for her to forgive him.

'I want to go home, Tariq,' she said, hanging on to the last of her dignity.

'You are my wife and you are not going anywhere.'

One glance at the rigid set of his hard, handsome features told her that argument was useless. For some reason he wanted her here. And you didn't have to be a genius to know what that reason was.

The sparks in his eyes, the sexual awareness that even now pulsed between them, all gave her the answer to that question.

She sucked in a breath, suddenly knowing what had to be done. *What would hurt him most.* 'You want me to stay? Fine, I'll stay. You thought you were going to have to endure forty days and forty nights with me, Tariq,' she breathed, 'and that's what you're going to do. You've proved that the only things that interest you in life are power, money and sex. Finally I understand the person you really are. You're right when you say the chemistry between us is powerful. You're right when you say that our wedding night was amazing. It was. But that was it. That was all you're ever going to get from me. From now on you can look, but you're not going to touch. Prepare yourself for forty days and forty nights of hell, Your Excellency.'

CHAPTER NINE

'WHAT do you mean, you can't find her?' Tariq paused in the act of prowling the length of his apartment, his dark eyes fierce, evidence of his usual self-control distinctly lacking. When she'd promised him hell, he hadn't anticipated that her first move would be to disappear.

Cold, hard logic told him that her unfortunate discovery of the truth had no bearing on the outcome of the deal. They were married. The shares were already his.

Mission accomplished.

So why did he suddenly feel as though his entire life was unravelling?

He was in the grip of emotions hitherto unknown to him. He was a man who had never in his life felt the need to explain his actions to anyone and yet suddenly he was filled with a burning need to explain every tiny detail. But the only person he wanted to explain himself to couldn't be found and the knowledge that she'd been *extremely* distressed immediately before she'd disappeared only served to increase his state of unease. Frustration and concern mingled with a severe attack of conscience.

Hasim Akbar clasped his hands together. 'She appears to have vanished, Your Excellency.'

Blasted out of his usual cool by that less than helpful statement, Tariq rounded on him. 'It is impossible for anyone to make a move in this palace without at least ten people witnessing the event. She must be somewhere. *Find her.*'

On the receiving end of that icy tone, Hasim tensed. 'No one has seen her since she left the audience chambers.'

The less than subtle reminder that he was the cause of the current situation left Tariq on the point of explosion.

'Find her,' he repeated in a soft, lethal voice that had Hasim backing towards the door. 'I want every corner of the palace searched, I want guards out on the streets. If necessary get helicopters up in the air. No one rests until her whereabouts are discovered.'

She'd been *very* upset when she'd left him. She could have wandered out of the Palace and into the seedier parts of Fallouk. *She could be in extreme danger.*

As the list of potential disasters lengthened in his mind, Tariq started to pace again, pausing only briefly to question precisely *why* his anxiety levels were running so high.

It was obvious, he told himself. Despite what she thought about him, he wasn't such a louse that he enjoyed seeing a distressed woman leave his Palace with absolutely no knowledge of the surrounding area.

Someone needed to find her.

Faced with the prospect of idleness or, worse still, introspection, he decided to join in the search himself.

Farrah sat curled up in the corner of one of the stables, indifferent to the future appearance of the long silk dress she was wearing. Her high heeled shoes had been discarded and lay half buried in the straw and she'd removed the pins from her blond hair, allowing it to fall loose down her back.

It was dark, it was late and she'd cried so hard that she didn't dare imagine what her face looked like. Given that she was only sharing the stable with a horse, she didn't see that it mattered.

The reminder that she was no longer dressing for a prince

brought fresh tears to the surface and she brushed them away with an impatient hand. Enough crying, she told herself firmly. *Enough*.

Eventually she'd get over him. It wasn't possible to hurt like this for ever. And in the meantime she was going to give him forty days and forty nights of total celibacy. For a man as red-blooded and virile as Tariq, knowing how much he wanted her in his bed again, being deprived of sex would be a just punishment.

But, before she could face returning to the Palace, she needed to allow herself the self-indulgence of a good cry.

She deserved that, at least.

'I suppose you think I'm mad,' she muttered to the pretty Arab mare who was munching through a pile of hay. 'Making a fool of myself again, over the same man. I'm obviously not great at learning lessons. And it's not just me—' tears welled again '—I've lost my dad his company because I was too blind and stupid to check exactly what marriage to Tariq would mean.' Would her dad be able to sort things out? If she hadn't been so miserable, she would have laughed because the one person in the world who was probably a match for Tariq was her father.

The horse turned her head and blew gently through her nostrils.

'I just feel like a total idiot,' Farrah confessed softly, curling her long legs underneath her. 'I thought Tariq loved me. I know he's arrogant and controlling but he really can't help that and I felt sorry for him because he's obviously had a pretty grim childhood. I thought I could teach him to be more demonstrative.'

The mare stamped her foot and dragged some more hay into her mouth.

'It turned out that the reason he wasn't demonstrative was because he didn't love me and, frankly, I don't believe he's capable of loving anyone,' Farrah said flatly, leaning her head back against the wall and closing her eyes. All the anger had drained out of her, leaving her limp and exhausted and unable to make a decision about anything. 'I just can't believe that I was such a gullible, stupid fool that I let the same man hurt me twice.'

The horse gave a whicker of sympathy and nuzzled Farrah's hand.

She opened her eyes and stroked the mare's velvety nose. 'I don't honestly know what I'm supposed to do now,' she mumbled. 'I don't have a single friend in this place. No one I can talk to. His family all loathe me. My dad's working on some project in the back of beyond so I can't get hold of him either and warn him what's happening. My life's a total mess.'

'Your life is *not* a mess, my family certainly doesn't loathe you and you can talk to me. In fact, I wish you would.' The deep, masculine tones were drawn tight with stress and she shrank back against the wall as Tariq walked into the stable and bolted the door behind him in a decisive movement that ensured that she wouldn't be escaping in a hurry.

Farrah flinched as she heard the finality of the clunk. She would sooner be trapped with scorpions and snakes. 'What are you doing here? I don't want to talk to you because you're a truly *horrible* person. Go away.'

Picking up the tension, the mare threw up her head and stamped her foot and Tariq reached out and stroked a soothing hand down her neck, his touch skilled and gentle.

Manipulative rat, Farrah thought dully as she watched him calm the horse with a few soft words and the gentle caress of his long fingers. Wasn't that exactly what he'd done to her? He'd soothed and charmed until he'd had her exactly where he wanted her.

'Have you any idea what an uproar you've caused?' Tariq demanded in a tense, driven tone. 'We have been searching for you for hours. The entire palace guard is out looking for you.'

It occurred to her that she'd never seen him look anything less than suave and well groomed. But tonight he looked anything but. He was dressed in the same suit he'd worn for his meeting with the Kazbanian foreign minister, but the jacket and tie had long since been discarded and what had started life as a crisp white shirt was now crumpled and dirtied. She wondered what he'd been doing. 'Why are the palace guard looking for me?'

'Because you vanished from the face of the earth. We needed to know where you were. I thought you might have had an accident. I was worried about you.' He frowned slightly, as if that confession was as much of a surprise to him as it was to her.

'Worried about your investment, you mean. But it wouldn't have mattered if I had had an accident, would it, Tariq? You've got what you want. You married me and the shares are yours.'

He sucked in a breath. 'Whatever you may think, this is *not* about the shares.'

'Of course it is.'

He dragged a hand through his glossy dark hair and glanced around him in disbelief. 'I can't believe we're having this conversation in my stables in the middle of the night. Come with me now and we'll talk.'

She didn't move. 'I don't want to talk. And I'll come when I'm ready and not before.'

'You mean you don't want to talk to *me*.' A muscle worked in his jaw and there was a wry gleam in his dark eyes. 'You've been talking to my horse quite happily for the past hour.'

She wondered just how much he'd overheard and then decided that it didn't matter. She'd already made an utter fool of herself over him. It really couldn't get any worse. 'I happen to like your horse.'

He gave her a curious look, momentarily distracted by her comment. 'I never knew you liked horses.'

'What difference would it have made?' she snapped. 'You weren't remotely interested in me as a person, were you, Tariq? You just wanted to manoeuvre me into marrying you and once I did that the rest was all irrelevant.'

'If that is the case, then why am I standing here now?'

'Damage limitation?' She leaned her head back against the wall and studied him in the dim light of the stable. 'You're a man who hates emotions. You've probably seen more today than in your entire lifetime. I'm sure you just want it all to go away. As you just pointed out, your normally ordered palace is in an uproar and you wanted to find me before I could disturb any more of your meetings.'

'Certainly the foreign minister of Kazban has rarely been so thoroughly entertained at my expense,' Tariq admitted with a rare display of humour. 'And what I really want is not for you to disappear but to come back to our apartment so that we can talk properly. It's freezing in here, you're wearing next to nothing and you cannot spend the night in my stables.'

'Why not? They're nice stables. And your palace is full of rats.' She gave him a pointed look and saw his eyes flash dark.

'We can work this out.'

'I don't think so.' She tilted her head to one side, her slightly sarcastic tone hiding layers of pain. 'This time you've really excelled yourself. But it doesn't matter, does it? Because you were never thinking about me, only yourself. It's what you're really, really good at.' Her voice rose and the mare threw up her head in alarm and stamped her foot.

Tariq put a reassuring hand on the horse's neck and turned back to Farrah.

'Are you going to be reasonable?'

'Probably not. I don't feel reasonable. If you really want to know, I feel stupid and gullible,' she threw at him. 'Discovering that you've been thoroughly manipulated isn't really the best incentive to be reasonable.'

But she was starting to shiver and felt his gaze fix on the tiny bumps that appeared on her skin.

'That's enough discussion. Being angry with me is no reason to risk pneumonia. You can sulk and ignore me in our apartments as easily as you can ignore me here,' he pointed out, stooping and sweeping her into his arms without further attempt at negotiation.

'I never sulk. And I want you to put me down,' she muttered, pushing at his chest, feeling the hard muscle under her fingers. 'You're always dragging me off. You need to learn the art of conversation instead of kidnap. And I don't want to be married to you anymore. I don't like you.'

'You're married to me and that's the way it's staying,' Tariq said grimly, tightening his grip on her as he strode from the stable. 'And I think this is one of those occasions when you should probably stop talking.'

'Why?'

'Because you might say something you'll regret later.'

'Offhand, I can't think of a single thing that I'd regret saying to you. The only thing I regret is the part where I said "I do",' she muttered but he simply tightened his grip and strode across a courtyard and through another door.

She was dimly aware of people staring and bowing but Tariq ignored them all, taking the stairs two at a time with her still in his arms.

At any other time she might have admired his impressive athletic ability, but now she simply glared at the hard ridge of his darkened jaw, which was within her line of vision.

'Don't you want to throw a bag over my head in case anyone spots that we've been having a row?'

A muscle worked in that same jaw. 'I'm not interested in anyone else's opinion. I am, however, interested in getting you out of that non-existent dress before you catch your death. The nights here are very cold and you're wearing very little.'

'It's not like you to complain about that, Tariq,' she said sarcastically just as he reached the door of his apartment.

Guards snapped to attention but Tariq ignored them, striding through the door with her still in his arms and kicking it shut behind him. He carried on walking, through the three luxurious and ornate living rooms, down a marble corridor and into the huge master bedroom, dominated by a massive bed.

A bed that she hadn't even had the chance to share with him yet.

And never would, she told herself firmly, ignoring the sudden rush of awareness that engulfed her as he deposited her firmly in the middle of the large bed. There was no misinterpreting the purposeful gleam in his eyes as he lifted a hand and unbuttoned his rumpled shirt.

'Don't even think about it, Tariq,' she warned, scooting up the bed out of reach of those dangerous, skilful hands.

He dropped the shirt on to the floor, his eyes still locked on hers. 'Why deny yourself what you know you want? The chemistry between us is all that matters here.'

The sight of his bronzed muscular chest was almost enough to make her believe him. Almost, but not quite.

'Yes, well, it would make it very convenient for you if I believed that. You think that everything can be solved by sex, but it can't,' she muttered, ignoring the banging of her heart and the buzz in her ears.

Rat, she reminded herself as she dragged her gaze away from the fascinating sight of dark, masculine body hair that followed a trail down his body and disappeared temptingly beneath the waistband of his trousers. *Neverland*, she thought to herself. She never should have gone there. *Major rat.*

As he reached for the button on his trousers she felt her blood heat and knew that urgent action was necessary to prevent her from doing something that she was going to sincerely regret later. Sliding off the bed, she made a run for the bathroom without giving him a chance to stop her. Pushing the lock home, she leaned against the door and slid slowly on to the cold marble floor.

Forty days and forty nights, she reminded herself.

She was going to make him suffer for forty days and forty nights.

And then she'd go home and spend the rest of her life trying to get over him.

* * *

Apart from fulfilling her role in certain social engagements, she devoted her time to avoiding Tariq.

She spent her nights dozing fitfully behind a locked door in the large dressing room that was part of the master suite. The door was locked for her sake as much as his. She didn't trust herself to be around him and not give into temptation. He was so unbelievably sexy that it would have been all too easy to just forget what he'd done and sink into his arms. But she wasn't going to do it. And every time she felt remotely tempted to unlock that door, she reminded herself what he'd done to her and to her father.

She'd tried over and over again to contact her father to warn him what was happening but so far it had proved impossible to track him down and she was growing more and more anxious.

What was he going to say when he discovered what she'd done?

Trying to distract herself, during the day she explored Tariq's palace. She discovered secluded courtyards with hanging gardens and bubbling fountains, she found a library, stocked floor to ceiling with books, but her most important discovery was the one she'd made on that first night. His stables.

Over the days that followed, she got to know each and every one of his horses by name and personality. Deciding that as her marriage was a sham then so was her role as Queen, she found herself a pair of jodhpurs and a loose, comfortable T-shirt and spent her time riding and caring for his horses. And if his staff thought her behaviour in any way odd, they concealed it.

It was a week after they'd arrived in Fallouk that she heard a sound that was entirely familiar to her. The uncontrolled yells of a child in the middle of a major temper tantrum. Acting on instinct, she put down the body brush she'd been using to groom the Prince's favourite stallion, left the stable and went to investigate.

Tariq's aunt was standing looking frustrated and out of her depth while a boy of about seven years old lay on the pristine lawn in front of the stables and drummed his heels into the ground. His jaw was clenched, his arms and legs rigid as they flew up and down, threatening damage to anyone daring to approach.

'If you cannot control yourself then I will leave you here until you can!' Tariq's aunt turned away from the boy, saw Farrah and quickly controlled her expression. But not before Farrah had seen the sadness and the desperation in her eyes. She recognized the look because she'd seen it in the eyes of other parents.

She knew immediately that there was more to the boy's behaviour than just an ordinary temper tantrum. Unsure of what to say, Farrah stood for a moment but Tariq's aunt merely straightened her shoulders defensively.

'Rahman suffers from behavioural problems,' she said stiffly. 'He is very difficult to handle. He must be left to come out of his temper by himself. Whatever you do, don't touch him. He hates being touched. It makes him worse.' And with that she walked off, leaving the child on the grass, screaming.

Farrah let out a sigh of disbelief, shook her head and dropped onto her knees next to the boy. She wouldn't touch him, but at least she could keep him company. 'If it's any consolation, this place makes me feel like screaming too,' she muttered but Rahman took no notice because he was making too much noise to hear her.

Farrah sat quietly, her mind absorbed, remembering a child with similar problems who had been sent by the family doctor to the riding stable where she worked.

The animals had helped him—really helped.

Looking at the boy now, she wondered whether anyone had ever taken him near the stables. Certainly there were several ponies in Tariq's stable with the right temperament to carry a child. Wasn't it worth a try?

She pondered the problem through an incredibly boring formal dinner that evening and when, the next morning, she found Rahman screaming on the grass again she made up her mind. What was there to lose?

And so Rahman became her project.

She took him with her to the stables every day. At first he just sat, silent and uncommunicative, on a pile of straw, watching while she tended the horses. Farrah took to grooming the quietest, most docile pony in the stables on a daily basis and eventually held out the brush to Rahman in silent invitation. He stared at her for a long moment and then he reached out and took the brush.

'Circular movements,' she said calmly, 'like this—' She demonstrated what she meant and then stood back, careful not to crowd him.

Tentatively he started to groom the pony himself, his movements growing more and more confident.

Several days later, she persuaded one of the grooms to help her take him for his first ride and Rahman smiled—really smiled.

And eventually the temper tantrums lessened, just as she'd hoped they would. She watched in satisfaction one morning as he hugged and stroked the pony.

'He really likes that,' she said quietly. 'Hugs are very important.'

'I'm glad you think so,' came a deep, drawl from behind her and she turned to find Tariq standing there, a sardonic expression in his dark eyes. 'You seem to have taken up permanent residence in my stables—' His voice tailed off as he noticed Rahman and he gave a sharp intake of breath. For a moment he watched while the boy fussed over the pony and then his jaw tightened. 'Farrah. I need to talk to you. Immediately.'

Worried that his icy tone would upset Rahman, Farrah slid out of the stable without arguing, moving just far away enough that they couldn't be overheard but not so far that she couldn't see the boy.

'What's the matter now?' Her tone was flippant. 'Share price dropped? Oil wells gone up in flames?'

'Get the child out of the stable now. He shouldn't be in there.'

Affronted by what she saw as a totally unreasonable command, Farrah opened her mouth to argue but then saw the look of concern in his eyes. He was worried. Which was something in his favour at least, she thought to herself.

'Rahman's fine. He's great with the horses.'

'How well do you know him? If he loses his temper he will frighten them and they might hurt him,' Tariq said quietly and she nodded.

'Yes, I'm sure you're right. But he doesn't lose his temper around the animals. I've seen it before. Children often relate to the horses in a way that they just can't seem to relate to adults. It's amazing really.'

His eyes narrowed. 'What do you mean, you've seen it before? When have you ever come across a child like Rahman?'

She hesitated. She was so used to hiding that part of herself. But why not tell him the truth? The time for games was long over. 'All the time, actually. I work in a riding stable and children with different disabilities are sent to us from all around. The horses can't always help, of course—' she gave a tiny shrug '—but mostly they do. It's amazing to watch. We have children who have never been able to move under their own steam before and then we put them on a pony and you see their little faces as they walk across the yard for the first time—' She broke off and blinked, aware that Tariq was looking at her with a strange expression in his eyes.

'You work with children?'

'Well, I work with the horses, really,' she confessed, pushing her hair out of her eyes. 'My talent is knowing which horse will be good with each rider. I don't pretend to be an expert on anyone's medical condition. There are other people who do that. I just do the pony bit. Horses have personalities, you know that, just like humans. Some of them are kind and they seem to sense whether they have to be gentle or not. They're so clever. That pony of yours over there—' she gestured with her hand to where Rahman was still grooming '—he's wonderful. Just the right type.'

'I bought him for one of my little cousins but she was never interested,' Tariq said and Farrah shrugged.

'Oh, well, her loss, Rahman's gain, I suppose. Is he your nephew?'

Tariq nodded. 'Yes. He has seen an endless round of doctors and psychologists and none of them have been able to cure his terrible rages. It seems you've managed to do in a matter of weeks what specialists have failed to do in years.'

Feeling suddenly awkward, Farrah rubbed the toe of her boot along the ground. 'Not me, the horses.'

Tariq breathed out heavily. 'How often do you work in the stables?'

'At home?' She looked up at him. 'Every day. I get there at five-thirty and I leave after the last child has gone. It's a pretty long day, but I love it.'

'You work in a stable every day?' He said the words slowly, as if he was having trouble comprehending and she nodded.

'Apart from Sundays. And I even go in on Sundays if they're really desperate.'

'And you didn't think this was something worth mentioning to me?'

'No. It's a part of my life I don't share with anyone. It embarrassed my mother because she could never understand why I'd rather be up to my knees in mud than dressed in designer heels. I'm sure you're equally embarrassed, but actually I don't care.' She lifted her chin defensively. 'I do it because I enjoy it and because I'm useful.'

He ran a hand over the back of his neck, a strange light in his eyes. 'We told each other many things in the desert and yet you didn't think to mention it.'

'Well, you didn't think to mention that we were only getting married for forty days and forty nights, so you can't really accuse me of keeping secrets,' she pointed out, moving back towards the stable.

He grabbed her hand in an iron grip. 'You are the most contradictory, infuriating woman I've ever met.'

'And I bet you've met a few, so that's probably a compliment. I need to check on Rahman—' She yanked her hand away from him and walked back into the stable, murmuring quiet words of praise to the boy and the horse, aware that Tariq was watching, simmering quietly from the other side of the stable door.

She could feel his gaze burning into her back as she took the brush from the boy.

'Time for your ride, I think. Let's saddle him up, shall we?'

She waited for Tariq to become bored and leave but instead he followed her out to the paddock she'd been using to give Rahman lessons.

'Don't you have anywhere to be?' Holding the pony's reins, she shot him an exasperated look. 'War could break out while you're hanging around here with me.'

'War is undoubtedly going to break out if I don't have five minutes alone with you soon,' Tariq promised in an undertone and she felt her heart jump in her chest.

'Forget it.'

'You are such a little hypocrite,' he breathed in a menacing tone. 'You want *exactly* what I want but you pretend otherwise.'

'I don't want anything, Tariq, except to go home.' And with that she walked the horse forward, ending the conversation.

She concentrated on Rahman and the pony and when she turned round again Tariq had gone. She should have been relieved that he'd finally left her alone, but instead she felt—disappointed?

Which just went to show that she was as stupid about the man as ever, she thought, turning her attention back to the boy and the pony.

She went through her day feeling more miserable than ever and after Rahman had left for the day she stayed on in the stables because she couldn't face going back to the Palace.

She completely lost track of the time and when she glanced up and saw Tariq standing in the doorway she blinked in astonishment. He was dressed in a dark grey suit that seemed only to emphasize the athletic perfection of his powerful frame. His hair shone dark and glossy under the harsh stable lights and his arrogant features showed evidence of strain.

'Tonight was the formal dinner to welcome the Crown Prince of Kazban,' he informed her helpfully and she felt a stab of guilt which she pushed away.

'If I was supposed to be there, then I'm sorry. I lost track of time.'

'Obviously.'

'Was I supposed to be there?'

'You're my wife. I married you.'

'Well, not really—' She pulled a face and turned back to the pony she was grooming. Anything to stop her looking at him. He was spectacular, she thought weakly. Stunning. Gorgeous. Virile. Masculine. Ignoring the slow curl of heat low in her pelvis, she closed her eyes briefly and talked sense into herself. Rat. Bastard. 'You married my shares. And I sort of came along too, which must have been pretty inconvenient for you.'

With a harsh expletive that she didn't understand, he crossed the stable and yanked her away from the pony. 'Enough.' His voice was a low, throaty growl as he powered her against the wall and trapped her there with the strength and heat of his body. 'I have heard enough. You are determined to simplify the complicated and soon we are going to talk about that, but for now I've had enough of talking and I've had enough of being patient. I have given you space to calm down and be reasonable and it hasn't happened.'

'Let me go, Tariq—' Overwhelmed by his masculine scent, the

fire in his eyes, *the sheer closeness of him*, she pushed at his hard chest, struggling against a temptation so large and potentially dangerous that her movements became frantic. 'Let me go—'

'No way—'

'Oh, God, don't do this to us—to me—' She wriggled against him in an attempt to free herself and then gave a soft moan as she felt the hard ridge of his arousal and the warmth of his breath as his mouth closed in on hers.

'You are the most *infuriating* woman.' His arms planted either side of her, blocking her escape, Tariq's voice was husky and seductive. 'I don't know whether to strangle you or kiss you.'

'Strangle me, definitely—it will be better for both of us,' Farrah gasped, her heart pounding hard against her ribs, her head swimming. 'I don't want you to kiss me. I really, *really* don't want you to kiss me—'

If he kissed her she'd be lost. If he kissed her, she'd—

His mouth came down on hers with punishing force, his kiss ravenous and desperate, trapping her sob of need. His hands slid down her arms and lifted them to his neck. He wanted her to cling and she clung, her arms wrapped round his powerful shoulders, her own shoulders pressed hard against the wall by the power of his body and the force of his passion.

She forgot that she didn't want him to kiss her. She forgot that this man had hurt her. She forgot that she'd resolved to keep her distance. She forgot *everything* except the fact that she'd kept her distance for two long weeks and now she needed him. She needed him badly.

His kiss was savage, a primitive assault on her senses that destroyed all thought and will power. Excitement whipped through her body like a loose electric wire as he stole and plundered, his body hard against hers until all she could feel was the pumped up, insistent throb of pulsing masculinity.

She felt his hand slide up to cup her breast and she arched in a desperate plea for more. Responding to her silent demand, he used both hands to jerk her shirt open in a rough, impatient gesture that sent buttons flying and made the pony throw up her head in alarm. But neither of them were aware of their surroundings. They were aware only of each other. Of the pounding hammering of hearts and the frantic lock of seeking mouths.

'I need you naked,' Tariq groaned, his hands swift and determined as he stripped her of the rest of her clothes and she was so completely desperate for him that she did nothing but urge him on. Her entire focus became the insistent, throbbing ache deep within her body that grew to monumental proportions and threatened to drive her mad with frustration.

Need made her uncoordinated and she clawed at his suit, groaning in frustration when her fingers met fabric instead of flesh.

When she felt his mouth on her bare breast she closed her eyes and gasped at the sheer perfection of the feeling and when she felt his strong fingers slide between her legs she gave a moan of frustration because his touch brought her so close to ecstasy and yet not close enough.

The hard, cold wall of the stable pressed against her bare back but she was oblivious to everything but her body and his. *Her need and his.*

Frantic for him, she reached down and fumbled with his zip and he covered her hand with his and helped her with the task. He was painfully aroused and so hot and hard that her entire body throbbed with an urgency so monumental that nothing could have stopped the inevitable.

Her desperation bordered on the indecent but she didn't even care.

'Now, Tariq—' her voice was strangled '—now, please—'

His eyes glinted dark, his breathing was harsh and he lifted her without hesitation, wrapped her legs around him and entered her with a hard, possessive thrust that brought a sob of pleasure and relief to her lips.

She felt the force of him deep inside her as he took her with barely contained violence and she moved her hips and clung to him as excitement surged through her body, caring for nothing except the need which grew and grew from deep within.

He thrust deep and he did it again and again until her vision blurred and her entire body exploded in a shower of sensation so exquisitely perfect that for a moment she ceased to breathe. She felt him shudder as he reached his own desperate climax and then there was only the slow descent back to normality. The unsteady breathing. The sudden intrusion of the outside world into their private place. The cold wall. The rhythmic munching of the pony in the corner of the stable…

Dazed and disorientated, it was only as he lowered her gently to the ground that Farrah realized that, although she was totally naked, he was fully clothed. Even his stylish silk tie was still in place.

For some reason, this stark reminder that she'd thought about nothing but her own need for him increased her mortification and she stopped quickly and retrieved the remains of her torn shirt. Head bowed, fingers shaking, she slipped it on and reached for her trousers.

Tariq caught her arm, his eyes dark and stormy, his breathing less than steady. 'We *really* need to talk—'

And that was the one thing she didn't want to do.

He was going to tell her that they might as well stay together until such time as he grew bored with her. Wasn't that more or less what he'd offered her five years before? A place in his bed until he decided that it was time to fill it with someone different?

Perfect mistress material—

Well, that wasn't what she wanted. What they shared was too powerful, but it was just sex, and sex wasn't enough for her. She couldn't live with him, knowing that he'd divorce her when the time was right. *When it suited him.*

Eventually he'd get bored with the sex and then where would

she be? In love with a man who didn't return her feelings and she couldn't live with that.

He *had* to let her go. That had been his plan all along and he probably wanted it even more now that he realized that she wasn't the person he'd thought she was.

So she'd leave and make it easy for him.

CHAPTER TEN

THE following morning, Farrah went in search of Asma.

She was drinking coffee and looking at dress designs and seemed more than a little disconcerted to see Farrah standing in the doorway.

'I'll come straight to the point.' Farrah closed the door so that their conversation couldn't be overheard. 'I want to leave this place, but I can't do it on my own so you're going to have to help me.'

Asma closed the book and gave her a cold look. 'Why would I help you?'

'Because you don't want me here and you never did,' Farrah pointed out and Asma gave a tiny shrug.

'I don't think—'

'Good, because you don't need to think,' Farrah said pleasantly. 'I just need you to find a reliable way of transporting me to the border with Kazban without Tariq knowing anything about it.'

The book fell from her hands. 'You're going to cross the border?'

'Once I'm in Kazban, I'll persuade the authorities to let me fly home,' Farrah explained impatiently. 'I can hardly just take a commercial flight out of Tazkash, can I?'

'I suppose not. You're seriously leaving?'

'That's right. And I want to do it quickly. You're his cousin. You must be able to arrange something. I just need transport, that's all, and a driver who knows the way.'

She had no intention of repeating the fiasco of the desert.

Asma's breathing quickened, as though she couldn't quite believe her luck. 'I—yes, I could, of course, but—'

'Good, that's settled, then. Tariq is tied up in meetings with the Prince of Kazban all day. I want to be gone long before he comes looking for me.'

Asma rose to her feet. 'I'll order a car for you. It will be outside the stable gates one hour from now.'

'Good.'

Which left only one further thing to do before she left.

Farrah returned to Tariq's apartment and found her bag. Inside was an envelope she'd had sent out from England only two days earlier.

She opened it up and stared at the contents, her eyes filling with tears. Then she blinked them away, picked up a pen and got to work.

The journey was smooth and without incident.

Farrah told herself that she was hugely relieved that Tariq hadn't chosen to leave his meeting early and hadn't suspected anything. She wouldn't have wanted him to follow her. She really, really wouldn't.

So why was it that no sooner did she brush away one tear, another one took its place?

She stared out across the dark gold dunes, which stretched into the distance, wondering if she'd ever see the desert again. Probably not. She wouldn't be coming back to Tazkash for a third time, that was for sure.

The knowledge that she might never see the place again left her unutterably depressed and she was so lost in thought that it took her a few moments to realize that they were slowing down.

When she finally noticed the buildings along the road and the men in uniform, she leaned forward in her seat with a frown. 'What's going on?'

'We've reached the border between Tazkash and Kazban,' came the reply and for some reason his words simply increased her misery.

So this was it, then.

Once they drove past those guards, Tariq would be in a different country, far away from her. Oh, why was she kidding herself? She brushed the tears away angrily. Tariq had always been far away from her. He was from a different country, a different culture—he was in a different league. They'd never stood a chance. All they shared was passion and that just wasn't enough.

She was about to look back at the majestic dunes for a final time when her door was jerked open and a uniformed guard stared down at her.

'Passport.' His face was hard and unsmiling and she felt a flicker of disquiet as she rummaged in her bag and handed over the document.

He took it from her and gestured for her to get out of the car. 'Come with me.'

Farrah did as he ordered, wondering whether this was a routine happening at the border.

He led her into the stone building and then stood to one side to let her pass. 'In there.'

Wondering what was going on, she walked into the room as he'd instructed and then stopped in shock. The door closed behind her but she wasn't even aware of that fact.

Tariq stood by a desk in the middle of the room, dressed in another sleek designer suit, his handsome face taut with strain. 'Must I keep you locked up? Every time I turn my back on you, you run away. *Why?*'

She found her voice. 'What are you doing here?'

'Abandoning my royal duties, as usual,' he said in a raw, impatient tone. 'If I wasn't the one in charge I would have been fired by now for taking so much time off. If you were to take your rightful place by my side as my wife, I might get a great deal more done in my working day.'

She curled her hands into her palms. 'My rightful place is not by your side. It was never meant to be like that, was it?'

'Why did you leave me these?' He threw the envelope on to the desk and she bit her lip.

'They're share certificates, Tariq. You married me for those. I hope you live happily ever after.'

She felt her voice crack and she turned towards the door, intending to leave before she made a complete fool of herself, but he moved so swiftly that she didn't even manage to take more than a step towards freedom.

'You're not going anywhere,' he said grimly, propelling her against the wall and trapping her there with his arms.

It reminded her of that incredible night in the stable and she felt tears threaten again.

'You married me for my shares, Tariq. Those are the shares and I just can't do this anymore. I'm leaving.'

'You're not leaving.'

'The shares are yours. You can divorce me. You don't even have to wait forty days and forty nights.'

'I won't be divorcing you. Ever.'

'You're being ridiculous—'

His mouth moved closer to hers. 'You think what we share is ridiculous?'

'What we share is just sex, Tariq. And I'm not prepared to stay with you until you get bored with me.'

'Bored?' He laughed in genuine amusement. 'Bored? I would give much for the opportunity to become bored by your company, *laeela*. You tell me exactly how you feel; I doubt you will ever learn to filter what happens between your brain and your mouth and you are reliably unpredictable. Every time I turn my back you are escaping and now I discover that you have a completely secret life of which I know nothing. There are many words to describe our relationship, but boring is certainly not one of them.'

'I'm not good at palace life.'

'You haven't made any effort to become involved in palace life,' Tariq said quietly. 'And I can hardly blame you for that. On your first visit here, my relatives were horribly unkind to you and gave you advice that made you feel even more awkward and out of place and that caused me to misjudge you.'

She lifted her head and looked at him. 'You knew they did that?'

'At the time, no.' His tone was weary. 'I'm afraid that five years ago I had a great deal to occupy my mind. My father was seriously ill, the economic future of the country was under threat from different directions. The demands on my time were such that I didn't give any thought to your feelings whatsoever and for that I apologise. All I saw was that when you arrived at my palace you changed into a different person.'

'I was trying to please you. I was trying to be the person I thought you wanted me to be.'

His eyes gleamed with a certain wry humour. 'I'm aware of that now. And I'm also aware that you were led down the wrong path by my family.'

'How did you find out?'

He released her then and turned and paced back across the room. 'I was determined to discover who told you about the plan to divorce you after forty days and forty nights. It did not take a genius to trace it back to my own family. Asma has always been horribly indulged by my aunt.'

'Well, I'm sure when she's your wife she'll learn to behave herself,' Farrah muttered, sidling towards the door.

'The guards are instructed not to allow you to pass,' Tariq informed her pleasantly, 'so there's no point in attempting another of your escape bids until this conversation is finished. And Asma will never be my wife.'

'Does she know that?'

'She does now. I made a point of speaking to both her and my aunt and pointing out that the role is no longer vacant because I am married to you and that is the way it is staying. There will be no more misunderstandings from that quarter. And anyway, my aunt has revised her opinion of you since you have worked such a miracle with Rahman. You will find her eager to secure more of your help in that direction.'

Farrah closed her eyes. The heat in the room was intolerable and her head was throbbing after her sleepless night. 'Why would you want to stay married to me? Because the sex is good?'

'No, because you are the woman I want to spend the rest of my life with.'

'I embarrass you.'

'That's *not* true. Five years ago I was completely charmed by you and then we returned to the Palace and I saw a different side of you.' He hesitated and his mouth tightened. 'This does not reflect well on me, but I confess that I was concerned that you were like your mother, a concern that my relatives used to their advantage when they gave you such unfortunate advice on how to dress and behave.'

It was painful hearing it and yet at the same time his words created a flicker of hope inside her. He hadn't *wanted* her to be like her mother. 'So when you discovered that you would have to marry me you must have *hated* the idea—'

He ran a hand over the back of his neck, visibly discomfited. 'Marriage to *anyone* was never at the top of my wish list,' he said honestly, 'and I think I only agreed to it because I knew that a divorce was possible. I wasn't really thinking about you. I only thought about me. I realize that confession does me no credit,' he added hastily, 'but you have to understand that I had a completely false impression of you at that point. It didn't occur to me that a divorce would bother you at all.'

'So you came after me purely for business gain.'

His gaze was wary. 'You are making it sound very bad but that is all in the past and it is the future that matters. The future that I am determined that we will have together.'

Her heart stalled and she swallowed hard. It was time to be honest. 'You don't know me, Tariq. You have no idea who I am.'

'And whose fault is that?' He turned on her, his dark eyes flashing, his mouth grim. 'You accuse me of not knowing you, you are quick to blame me for all the faults in our relationship, but are you not at least partly to blame too? You were careful to keep so much of yourself hidden away. Think about it, Farrah.'

'You think I'm a lightweight party animal. You think that of all women. You think all we care about is hair and shoes.'

'Because up until now that has been true of the women I have had the misfortune to mix with. But you gave me no reason to question my own prejudices. In fact you chose to perpetrate that image, did you not?' One ebony brow lifted in challenge. 'Is it not true that you turn up at high society events looking like a million dollars and socialize?'

'Yes, but—'

'And you appear to be enjoying yourself. Do you advertise the fact that you were working with disadvantaged children in a grubby stable only minutes before you slip on your high heels?'

'No, but—'

'It is true that I'm perfect in many ways,' Tariq drawled in a slightly mocking tone, 'but even I have yet to perfect the art of mind-reading and it's time that you offered the odd explanation for your own behaviour in all of this. You placed certain facts in front of me. You built an image for yourself over the years. Why did you do that?'

Farrah swallowed. 'Because I was always a disappointment to my mother. She wanted a girly girl and instead she got me.

As I child I was overweight, clumsy and I loved being outdoors. I was useless at ballet but good at riding horses. I spent my teenage years treading a fine line between pleasing myself and pleasing her.' She took a deep breath. 'And I also changed my image because of you. When you told me that I wasn't good enough to be your wife, that was the final spur I needed to reinvent myself. You hurt me so badly that I thought I could put a protective shell between myself and the world and so, from then on, I lived two very different lives. And the glamorous socialite bit wasn't as empty and useless as it sounds. I raised lots of money for the charities I cared about.'

'And during the day you worked with horses and children.' He raised a brow in question. 'So, having heard that story, can you honestly blame me if I chose to believe the image you portrayed? I interpreted the facts as you presented them to me and was that not exactly what you wanted and expected people to do?'

Farrah stared at him. He was right, of course. She *did* present a certain image to the world. An image very different from her real self. In fact, she relished the fact that, even in such public times, she'd managed to keep a large part of herself so private.

'Wealth makes you suspicious of people and their motives.' She bit her lip as she made a feeble attempt to explain. 'My mother found the real me highly embarrassing so I've learned to hide who I am. I suppose I'm not used to trusting anyone with my secrets.'

'And neither am I. In that way, at least, we are similar.'

She'd never thought of it like that, but it was true. How could she blame him for forming the wrong opinion of her, when she herself had been at least partially responsible for giving him that opinion? 'Five years ago you invited me to be your mistress—'

'I was under a great deal of pressure at the time. My father was desperately sick but not so sick that he couldn't interfere with everything I was doing.' Tariq strode around the room, his expression fierce. 'My time in the desert with you was an oasis of calm in my life. I wanted you to stay with me but suddenly we returned to the Palace and everyone in the Kingdom found reasons why I should not be with you, reasons that you supported with your manner of dress and your behaviour.'

'It should have been about us, Tariq, not anyone else—'

'You have no idea how often I wished that to be the case. How often I wanted to heave the responsibility on to someone else and ride off with you, as we did for so many months on the beach. A man and a woman. You dreamed of Nadia and her Sultan and yet I was weighed down by the responsibility of running the country in my father's place. You saw everything as simple and yet, for me, the simple did not exist.'

She felt a stab of guilt and realized suddenly that, until that moment, she'd never really understood the monumental pressure that he'd been under. 'I only ever thought about our relationship,' she admitted, aware that she'd been hideously self-absorbed and selfish. 'I thought you were ignoring me.'

'I was up to my ears in palace politics, as you so accurately call it,' Tariq said dryly and Farrah blushed.

'And I was naïve. I admit it. I should have realized what Asma was doing, but I didn't have any confidence in myself. Have you any idea of what it is like to be just eighteen and in love with the sexiest man in the world?' She swallowed. 'My mother destroyed my confidence in myself and your palace was full of gorgeous women, far more sophisticated and worldly than me. There was no way I could compete.'

'But I did not want a woman who was sophisticated and worldly. I wanted you. Which is why, when the opportunity to come after you presented itself, I snatched it.' He walked over to her and took her hands in his and she stilled.

'What are you saying?'

He lifted her hands to his lips. 'I'm saying that even the need to gain control of your father's company wouldn't have been enough to tempt me into marriage unless that was what I wanted.'

Her heart pounded. 'But you needed my father's company.'

'That deal could have been achieved in other ways,' Tariq said quietly, still holding her hands tightly. 'The truth is when I was offered an excuse I grabbed it, not because of the shares but because I wanted to marry you. I only realized that myself recently.'

'You're just saying that because you're in a tight spot.' He was a master negotiator—she knew that and she'd made a fool of herself over this man twice. She wasn't going to do it again.

'I told myself that I was marrying you for your father's shares because I was not ready to admit, even to myself, that my reasons could be more complex than that.'

'Tariq—'

'Don't interrupt me. I'm trying to say something I've avoided saying for my whole life and it isn't easy.' He released her hands and paced over to the other side of the room before turning back to face her. 'I love you. I married you because I loved you, although I don't think even I recognized it at the time, and I want to stay married to you because I love you. There, I've said it three times and it's getting easier already.' He gave a self-deprecating smile and for a moment she couldn't speak. Couldn't respond.

'You love me?'

'Unbelievable, isn't it?' He spread his hands in a fatalistic gesture. 'Finally I fall in love with a woman who loves me in return, but it is all in jeopardy because of my stupidity in linking our marriage with a business deal. How am I ever to convince you?'

She wasn't ready to give in that easily. 'How do you know that I love you in return?'

'You have always loved me,' Tariq said softly, 'but it has taken me a long time to recognize that too. You see, I'm not used to seeing love. My parents didn't love each other and none of the women I have been with have loved me any more than I loved them.'

'You married me intending to divorce me—'

'That may be true. But I made up my mind on our wedding night that I would *not* be divorcing you.'

'But Asma—'

'Our marriage is no one's business but our own.' He folded his arms across his chest and lifted an eyebrow. 'And now it seems to me that I've been doing a great deal of grovelling and apologizing for a Sultan and I'm hearing very little from you in return.'

That statement sounded so much like his usual arrogant self that she gave a slow smile, hope building inside her. 'What do you want to hear?'

'A declaration that you intend to stop running away? Something about you being crazy about me, loving me madly—' there was a glimmer of humour in his eyes '—that kind of thing.'

'We're different, Tariq—'

'A fact for which I am grateful on a daily basis,' he drawled, strolling towards her and dragging her into his arms. 'Enough argument. We *are* different, it's true. But we are supposed to be different. Different is good.'

'You're arrogant and stubborn—'

He gave a dismissive shrug. 'And you speak without thinking. It's part of the person you are and I love you for it.'

'You always command and order—'

He slid his hands either side of her face and dropped a gentle kiss on her mouth. 'And you are ridiculously, extravagantly, impractically romantic, but I love you for that too.'

She stared up at him. 'You don't know me—'

'I know everything you have allowed me to learn,' he said softly. 'I look forward to discovering the rest if you'll allow me to do so.'

'But—'

'I know that you love horses and children, that you are kind and giving. I know you like the simple life but are also comfortable at formal occasions. I know that politics and intrigue make you uncomfortable but I'll teach you how to cope with it. I know that you love our desert, enjoy our food and that you are not safe to drive on a sand dune.'

She gave a gasp of outrage. 'I drive well on sand!'

'You will, after more lessons,' he said confidently and she laughed.

'You're assuming I'm staying.'

'Why would you leave, when you know that you love it here? Despite what you think, you will not have to live your life in a goldfish bowl. There are many charities who would be glad of your help and there is a riding school within Fallouk where you could help if that would make you happy.'

'It wouldn't embarrass you?'

'On the contrary—' his voice was soft and there was a strange light in his eyes '—I never thought it possible to be so proud of my wife.'

She felt colour touch her cheeks. 'And your pipeline?'

Tariq released her and took a step backwards, his expression serious. 'The pipeline is a crucial project. I spoke to your father a few days ago and explained everything to him. He was surprisingly reasonable, given the circumstances. I will no longer be taking over the company but we have agreed on a partnership that will benefit both parties.'

Relieved that her father's business was no longer in jeopardy, Farrah smiled. 'He's a man who understands love.'

Tariq nodded. 'Obviously. Now that you are my wife, he is coming here tomorrow to reopen discussions on how to proceed with the project. So all that remains is for you to decide what you are going to do when he arrives. Should you still wish to leave, I'm sure he would be happy to take you home. Alternatively, he can join us for some belated wedding celebrations.'

For the first time she saw uncertainty in his eyes and it was that uncertainty that made up her mind.

'I am home, Tariq.' She walked towards him and reached up to hug him. 'You know I love you—'

'Yes, I do know that.' Tariq's voice was unsteady. 'But I didn't know if you would be able to forgive me for the less than conventional route we took to reach this point.'

'The thing about love is that it's generous and forgiving,' she breathed, 'love is kind and everything good. And love can perform miracles.'

'That I know to be true.' Tariq leaned down, his mouth hovering temptingly close to hers, 'because I found you. And that truly is a miracle.'

'If I stay married to you, do I have to dress like a queen?'

'Only part of the time,' he promised in a husky, sexy drawl. 'The rest of the time you will be *undressed*—'

And with that he kissed her, leaving her in absolutely no doubt that as well as being generous, forgiving, kind and good, love was also perfect.

* * * * *

THE ROYAL HOUSE OF NIROLI
Always passionate, always proud

The richest royal family in the world—
united by blood and passion,
torn apart by deceit and desire

Nestled in the azure blue of the Mediterranean Sea, the majestic island of Niroli has prospered for centuries. The Fierezza men have worn the crown with passion and pride since ancient times. But now, as the king's health declines, and his two sons have been tragically killed, the crown is in jeopardy.

The clock is ticking—a new heir must be found before the king is forced to abdicate. By royal decree the internationally scattered members of the Fierezza family are summoned to claim their destiny. But any person who takes the throne must do so according to The Rules of the Royal House of Niroli. Soon secrets and rivalries emerge as the descendents of this ancient royal line vie for position and power. Only a true Fierezza can become ruler—a person dedicated to their country, their people...and their eternal love!

Each month starting in July 2007,
Harlequin Presents is delighted to bring you
an exciting installment from
THE ROYAL HOUSE OF NIROLI,
in which you can follow the epic search
for the true Nirolian king.
Eight heirs, eight romances, eight fantastic stories!

Here's your chance to enjoy a sneak preview of the first book delivered to you by royal decree...

FIVE minutes later she was standing immobile in front of the study's window, her original purpose of coming in forgotten, as she stared in shocked horror at the envelope she was holding. Waves of heat followed by icy chill surged through her body. She could hardly see the address now through her blurred vision, but the crest on its left-hand front corner stood out, its *royal* crest, followed by the address: *HRH Prince Marco of Niroli...*

She didn't hear Marco's key in the apartment door, she didn't even hear him calling out her name. Her shock was so great that nothing could penetrate it. It encased her in a kind of bubble, which only concentrated the torment of what she was suffering and branded it on her brain so that it could never be forgotten. It was only finally pierced by the sudden opening of the study door as Marco walked in.

"Welcome home, *Your Highness*. I suppose I ought to curtsy." She waited, praying that he would laugh and tell her that she had got it all wrong, that the envelope she was holding, addressing him as Prince Marco of Niroli, was some silly mistake. But like a tiny candle flame shivering vulnerably in the dark, her hope trembled fearfully. And then the look in Marco's eyes extinguished it as cruelly as a hand placed callously over a dying person's face to stem their last breath.

"Give that to me," he demanded, taking the envelope from her.

"It's too late, Marco," Emily told him brokenly. "I know the truth now…." She dug her teeth in her lower lip to try to force back her own pain.

"You had no right to go through my desk," Marco shot back at her furiously, full of loathing at being caught off-guard and forced into a position in which he was in the wrong, making him determined to find something he could accuse Emily of. "I trusted you…."

Emily could hardly believe what she was hearing. "No, you didn't trust me, Marco, and you didn't trust me because you knew that I couldn't trust you. And you knew that because you're a liar, and liars don't trust people because they know that they themselves cannot be trusted." She not only felt sick, she also felt as though she could hardly breathe. "You are Prince Marco of Niroli…. How could you not tell me who you are and still live with me as intimately as we have lived together?" she demanded brokenly.

"Stop being so ridiculously dramatic," Marco demanded fiercely. "You are making too much of the situation."

"*Too much?*" Emily almost screamed the words at him. "When were you going to tell me, Marco? Perhaps you just planned to walk away without telling me anything? After all, what do my feelings matter to you?"

"Of course they matter." Marco stopped her sharply. "And it was in part to protect them, and you, that I decided not to inform you when my grandfather first announced that he intended to step down from the throne and hand it on to me."

"To protect me?" Emily nearly choked on her fury. "Hand on the throne? No wonder you told me when you first took me to bed that all you wanted was sex. You *knew* that was the only kind of relationship there could ever be between us! You *knew* that one day you would be Niroli's king. No doubt you are expected to marry a princess. Is she picked out for you already, your *royal* bride?"

* * * * *

Look for THE FUTURE KING'S PREGNANT MISTRESS
by Penny Jordan in July 2007,
from Harlequin Presents,
available wherever books are sold.

He's proud, passionate, primal—
dare she surrender to the sheikh?

Feel warm winds blowing through your hair and the
hot desert sun on your skin as you are transported to
exotic lands.... As the temperature rises, let yourself be
seduced by our sexy, irresistible sheikhs.

Kidnapped by rebels, Belle Winters is rescued by
Sovereign Prince Rafiq. At his exotic palace, she is
astounded to learn that Rafiq expects her to show her
gratitude...by marrying him!

THE SHEIKH'S
RANSOMED BRIDE

by Annie West

(#2649)

On sale July 2007.

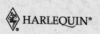

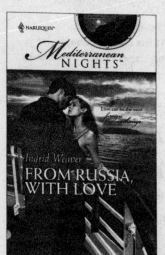

REQUEST YOUR FREE BOOKS!

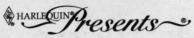 

2 FREE NOVELS PLUS 2
FREE GIFTS!

YES! Please send me 2 FREE Harlequin Presents® novels and my 2 FREE gifts. After receiving them, if I don't wish to receive any more books, I can return the shipping statement marked "cancel." If I don't cancel, I will receive 6 brand-new novels every month and be billed just $3.80 per book in the U.S., or $4.47 per book in Canada, plus 25¢ shipping and handling per book and applicable taxes, if any*. That's a savings of close to 15% off the cover price! I understand that accepting the 2 free books and gifts places me under no obligation to buy anything. I can always return a shipment and cancel at any time. Even if I never buy another book from Harlequin, the two free books and gifts are mine to keep forever.

106 HDN EEXK   306 HDN EEXV

Name _____ (PLEASE PRINT)

Address _____ Apt. #

City _____ State/Prov. _____ Zip/Postal Code

Signature (if under 18, a parent or guardian must sign)

Mail to the **Harlequin Reader Service®:**
IN U.S.A.: P.O. Box 1867, Buffalo, NY 14240-1867
IN CANADA: P.O. Box 609, Fort Erie, Ontario L2A 5X3

Not valid to current Harlequin Presents subscribers.

Want to try two free books from another line?
Call 1-800-873-8635 or visit www.morefreebooks.com.

* Terms and prices subject to change without notice. NY residents add applicable sales tax. Canadian residents will be charged applicable provincial taxes and GST. This offer is limited to one order per household. All orders subject to approval. Credit or debit balances in a customer's account(s) may be offset by any other outstanding balance owed by or to the customer. Please allow 4 to 6 weeks for delivery.

Your Privacy: Harlequin is committed to protecting your privacy. Our Privacy Policy is available online at www.eHarlequin.com or upon request from the Reader Service. From time to time we make our lists of customers available to reputable firms who may have a product or service of interest to you. If you would prefer we not share your name and address, please check here. ☐

HP07

Mediterranean Brides

**Two billionaires, one Greek, one Spanish—
will they claim their unwilling brides?**

Meet Sandor and Miguel, men who've taken all the prizes
when it comes to looks, power, wealth and arrogance.
Now they want marriage with two beautiful women.
But this time, for the first time, both Mediterranean
billionaires have met their matches and it will take more
than money or cool to tame their unwilling mistresses!

Miguel made Amber Taylor feel beautiful for the
first time. For Miguel it was supposed to be a
two-week affair…but now he'd taken the most
precious gift of all—her innocence!

TAKEN:
THE SPANIARD'S VIRGIN

Miguel's story (#2644)

by Lucy Monroe

On sale July 2007.

www.eHarlequin.com